IMAGINING

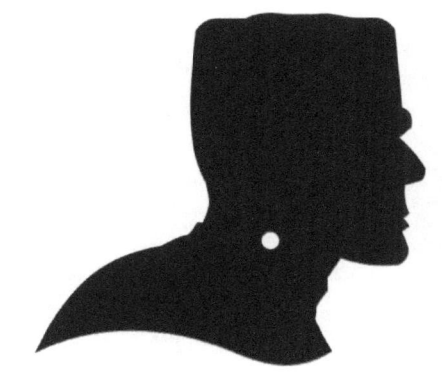

MONSTERS

IMAGINING MONSTERS

Lead Editor
Alison McBain

WestportWRITES Organizers
Alex Giannini & Cody Daigle-Orians

"The Chorus from the Hive" © 2019 by Edward Ahern
"The Wedding March" © 2019 by Elizabeth Chatsworth
"Monster" © 2019 by Gabi Coatsworth
"Shelter in Place" © 2019 by Cody Daigle-Orians
"You Get What You Pay For" © 2019 by Dave D'Alessio
"Smell the Rain" © 2019 by Alex Giannini
"Zombie Killer" © 2019 by Roman Godzich
"A Conversation Between Mother and Son" © 2019
    by Sheryl Kayne
"Monstrous Practices" © 2019 by P.C. Keeler
"Herstory" © 2019 by Alison McBain
"Valley Girls" © 2019 by V.P. Morris
"Annabelle" © 2019 by Marc Sirkin
"All Mind: The Influencers" © 2019
    by Corrine "Mitzy Sky" Taylor
"Furry Little Things on a Full Moon Night" © 2019
    by D.J. Whitney

ISBN-13: 978-1-949122-14-5 (Paperback)
ISBN-13: 978-1-949122-15-2 (eBook)

Front and back cover images and design by Shannon Stamey. Interior design by Alison McBain.

Fairfield Scribes—Fairfield, CT
WestportWRITES—Westport, CT
United States of America

First printing June 2019.
www.fairfieldscribes.com
westportlibrary.org/tags/westportwrites

This book is dedicated to
all the wonderful writers of Connecticut.

Contents

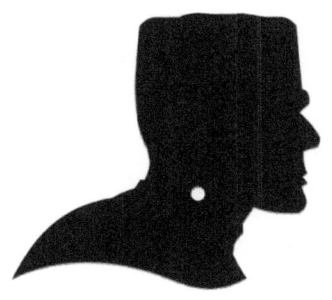

FOREWORD

IT'S APPROPRIATE THAT WE CELEBRATE the 200th anniversary of *Frankenstein* with an anthology of stories. Because, really, the creation of literature's most famous—and most enduring—monster was a shared experience, of sorts.

The idea? That was all Mary Shelley. But the spark, if you will, behind that idea? The spark was a communal experience, as a group of friends gathered in a castle on a dark and stormy night and challenged each other to tell ghost stories.

Shelley's ghost was a creature, stitched-together parts of the discarded and forgotten—a monster made of men—who stumbles into the darkness to face the world's monsters. Shelley's ghost lives on, these 200 years later, refusing death in a manner similar to her tragic, fictional doctor.

This, too, is utterly appropriate. Because the truth of writing, of being a writer, is very close to the truth of death. Like dying, we all must write alone. My thoughts, through my fingers, and out onto my page. Sure, we hope that eventually others will read what we've put down—sometimes through sheer force of will, sometimes through blood and tears, and sometimes, in those lovely and rare flashes of inspirational lightning, through a flurry of happy keystrokes.

No matter how the story kicks and screams its way into creation, though, the process is always the same and it is always, ultimately, lonely. We close the door to the study, or we pop on our headphones in a busy coffee shop, or we dictate into our phones as we navigate our evening commute.

But, as Shelley showed us all those years ago on that dark and stormy night tucked away in that castle in the countryside, sometimes it's okay to let others in. Share the story as it's being created. Surround yourself with other writers and maybe come away with something wholly unique.

That was one of the purposes of the book you now hold in your hands. It all started on a (dark, but quite lovely) Friday night at the Westport Library in Connecticut. Members of our WestportWRITES community gathered to hear about the history of *Frankenstein* and how the novel and its creations have permeated our culture for two centuries. And then, as writers tend to do, we wrote. Spread out through the library, clustered in small groups. Alone, but together. This collection is the result of that night, and of a partnership with the Fairfield Scribes and their fearless and wonderful leader, Alison McBain.

In these tales you'll meet ghosts old and new, monsters of all shapes and sizes. So venture forward. Meet these monsters. Hopefully, it's dark and stormy outside your castle.

> Alex Giannini & Cody Daigle-Orians
> The Westport Library

Zombie Killer

Roman Godzich

"MOTHER WARNED ME NOT TO do it," she said to the hideous head in the glass. "Become a gynecologist or a proctologist, she said. Something safe. But not an epidemiologist where you're dealing with those nasty, dangerous viruses. That's what she would say."

The ugly face grinned back at her, grunting.

"But I had to join the CDC. I could save the world one day. We were all so excited when we created this new virus. A way to inoculate people against fear. A game changer for people who live a life of hesitancy. Of course, we were shocked when the Pentagon wanted it for soldiers. We never imagined that. And we never imagined that every infected person would begin to see all the people around them as zombies. Still don't know why it works that way."

The face behind the glass lost an eyebrow and growled.

"And then the damned thing goes airborne. Ten thousand people infected in the first week. And they killed over two hundred thousand uninfected. Ten thousand berserkers acting like an insane army in the middle of Atlanta. Nobody is ever ready to fight off someone who is so crazy with fear that they kill anyone and everyone that they see. All those movies over the years. All those TV shows. They pretty much trained the infected to grab a weapon and start killing zombies."

The mottled face looked nervous. Almost as if it was trying to concentrate on something it could never comprehend.

She continued, "Sending in the police and the army was no use. It just created more highly armed, terrified killers. The death tolls skyrocketed."

The face smiled at that, a satisfied grin.

"We never found out if it was a natural mutation or part of trying to weaponize the virus. In the end, it didn't really matter, did it?"

The grisly head nodded in a familiar way.

"There might still be a few out there, a small number, who are immune to this thing. But they're not immune to their neighbors. They're being hunted. Not by mindless zombies, but by intelligent, terrified humans. I'm afraid they don't stand a chance."

The face coughed up a sickly green ooze that splattered the glass. It tilted its head, looking confused.

"It's the end," she said. "The end of everything. The end of humanity. And all because of assholes like you."

She lifted a large syringe and the monster backed away.

"Well, it's your time to die, you bitch."

She stabbed the syringe into her own arm and pressed the plunger. The cyanide did its work quickly. Her head shattered the mirror as she fell into it.

Monster

Gabi Coatsworth

"SO TELL ME. WHAT BRINGS you here?"

I always started with this. Even if my patients didn't think they knew, deep down they did, and this was a good way of getting them started. We'd performed the introductions, and she'd filled out the obligatory form, but I'd only glanced at it.

Joanna Martin sat perched on the edge of the sofa with the safety of the coffee table between us. She looked uncomfortable, as though her dowdy, neutral-colored clothes didn't fit right, but most people felt nervous the first time they saw a therapist. I made a couple of notes: Lacking in self-confidence. Mousy. Timid?

"I've been having dreams recently. Nightmares."

Her large, dark eyes, ringed with shadows, stared out of a pale face. She pushed a strand of lank brown hair behind one ear.

4

"Tell me what you recall about these dreams."

"That's the trouble. I can't remember what they're about. But I wake up suddenly in the night, sweating, and I know I've had one."

I decided to approach things from a different angle. Maybe this was just the beginning of menopause. She was about the right age, early fifties, I guessed.

"How long have you been having them?"

There was a pause. I remained silent, as I always do. People come to things in their own good time. Then she whispered something.

"I'm sorry, could you repeat that?"

She continued, voice barely above a whisper. "About six months or so. Since my mother died."

If I had a nickel . . .

"Tell me more about her," I said. I knew where this was going.

She told me all the usual stuff. Such a wonderful mother, such a great childhood, how sad now she was gone.

We made an appointment for the following week. When I finally checked the form she'd completed, I found she was only forty-eight.

This time, I noted she'd at least washed her hair before coming in, though a hairdresser could have improved it. Still, her coiffure wasn't my business.

"How have you been sleeping?"

Joanna was staring out of the window, avoiding my eyes, I thought. "Joanna?" She returned her gaze to me.

"Not much better," she said. "Perhaps worse."

"It's common when people are mourning the loss of a loved one to have problems getting a good night's sleep."

She gave a sort of bark. Had she just laughed?

Seeing my surprise, she began to explain, haltingly at first.

"My mother was very beautiful," she said.

Nothing unusual there. Lots of children saw their mother that way. I made a note, and nodded at her to continue.

"No, I mean genuinely good-looking. Kind of like Zsa Zsa Gabor."

I had to think a minute. Oh, right, the Hungarian film actress from the 50s and 60s. Blonde hair, pouty lips, high cheekbones. I could almost picture her, but couldn't remember much about her. I studied my client's face for a moment. Anyone less like a movie star was hard to imagine.

"What was it like, living with such an attractive mother?"

"It was okay, you know . . ."

"Tell me more."

"When I turned thirteen, I think, is when it started. She used to tell me I was a failure. She was right, of course. I got good grades at school, but I never *looked* the way she wanted me to."

"How so?"

"She always wanted me to be more glamorous. Go blonde, wear makeup and be more of a credit to her, I guess."

I studied her face, entirely makeup-free. But I couldn't assume she never wore any. Clients in a rush, or feeling depressed, would sometimes show up without their usual 'face.'

"Are you sure that's what she wanted?"

"Well, yes. Wouldn't you? Want your daughter to look lovely?"

I didn't answer the question. Some mothers, the narcissistic ones, didn't want to be outshone by their daughters. I didn't have to worry about that. I only had a son. But clearly she needed to figure this out.

"And how did you feel about that?" I continued

A fleeting expression of irritation passed across her face before vanishing, to be replaced by an attempt at a smile.

"I suppose you always have to ask. Well, I felt she was right, of course. I never was as beautiful as her." She paused. "She was obsessed with keeping her looks. She'd been a member of the Czech ballet, dancing in Italy when the war broke out. My father was in the Marines, on shore leave, and saw her. Quite quickly, she married him."

"Sounds like it was love at first sight." I knew that was most unlikely, but I wanted to see whether she regarded it that way.

"Oh, no. Absolutely not," she said vehemently. "She didn't want to go back to Czechoslovakia, what with the Germans marching in. So he was her ticket out. I don't think she ever loved him at all."

"Oh?"

She was on a roll now.

"I think life disappointed her. Living here wasn't what she expected. Daddy was a sweet man. Always kind to me. He could see she didn't like me much. But he wasn't what you might call a strong personality. She made it hard for him if he tried to stand up for me. She ruled the roost, until he left her in the end. I was out of the house by that time, thank God. He died a couple of years afterwards, so then it was only me and her."

"How did you handle that?"

"I did what I could to avoid her, of course. I got married." She lifted her chin as she looked at me. "We're getting a divorce."

Layers and layers of pain, I thought. The box of tissues was within reach, though at this moment, she didn't appear to need them.

"Do you want to talk about your relationship with your husband?"

"Not really. At least, not now. The marriage was a mistake. Apart from the kids. They're my pride and joy."

"Tell me about them next time," I said.

But the following Tuesday, she didn't mention the children at all. Her lips showed a smudge of pale pink lipstick, which brightened up her face, and the blouse she was wearing looked freshly ironed. But the dreams were still bothering her.

"I'm sorry to hear that." I waited for her answer.

"The problem is I'm beginning to remember what they're about."

She fell silent, and I could see she was struggling with something.

"I'm not having them quite so often, but, in the ones I can visualize, there's a huge woman following me. I try to escape her but I can't. Just as she's about to catch me, I see her face is disintegrating as she runs after me. And I wake up."

Seemed clear enough. Her mother's influence, or oppressive presence, was beginning to fade. I patted myself on the back. When therapy began to benefit the patient, I always felt my work was worthwhile.

"And what do you think this disintegration signifies?" It sometimes took a person quite a while to see the meaning of their dream. But not this time.

"It's my mother." She stopped, and tears started to well up. I handed her the box of tissues. "It's what actually happened to her."

I must have allowed my confusion to show.

"I told you she was obsessed with her appearance. About eight years ago, I think, she was turning sixty. She could easily have passed for someone in their forties—everyone said so. But she saw an ad in some magazine for a kind of therapy in Switzerland which promised to keep you young forever. So she contacted this Doctor Franck, and went off to his clinic for three weeks. She never talked about what the treatment entailed, except to say it wasn't a facelift. To cut a long story short, when she came back, I guess she did strike me as looking a bit younger."

"Was it very expensive?" Totally inappropriate question for a therapist. But I had to admit it sounded interesting.

"I think she cleared out the savings account to pay for the whole thing. I can't say for sure. But Dad was livid when he found out how much she'd spent. He told me so."

Too pricey for me. I refocused on her story.

"Anyway, all she would say when she came back was that the doctor had told her she had to 'stay warm.' I think that's when things started to go wrong."

"In what way?"

"She kept the temperature at eighty degrees or more, night and day, and if she went outside in winter, she'd wear a shawl draped around her face to preserve it."

"Was this a problem for you? You weren't living at home then, were you?"

"No. But when she came around, she'd insist we turn the heating up, even in summer. It got so we stopped inviting her. I'd go to visit her, but it was always stifling in the house. Unbearable."

Well, at least her case was interesting. I'd never had one quite like it. "I'm afraid our time is up for today. We'll talk more next week."

"I'm glad the weather's changing," I remarked when Joanna walked in. She'd added a little mascara, and her hair was shorter, with blonde highlights. She made for the sofa and sat back in it, more at ease, I thought. Good.

"I guess so. But warmer weather . . ."

I remembered her mother and her insistence on warmth.

"Of course," I said. "Would you like to carry on where you left off?"

It was like opening the floodgates.

"She kept her looks, all right, but it didn't make her happy. Whenever I came through the front door, she'd say, 'Lovely to see you darling. You look terrible.' " Joanna seemed unaware of the tears beginning to slide down her cheeks. "Not one word. Not one word of encouragement or praise. Why did I keep going back? I must have felt she needed me, but now I wonder."

She stopped to blow her nose, and sat up a bit straighter. A promising sign.

"My husband told me I shouldn't bother going to see her if it made me miserable, but he didn't understand. Men don't, do they?"

She looked at me as if waiting for an answer, but I don't think she really expected one, because she went on.

"She'd always find something to pick on. She was ill one time, only a heavy cold with a cough, so I took her some chicken soup I'd made. 'Not as tasty as mine. Why do I have such a daughter?' she said. And she was always criticizing my children. They weren't dressed properly, their manners were awful, and on and on." She stopped and her gaze drifted to the trees coming into bud outside the window.

"And how did you feel about this?"

"I suppose I was used to it, but I still don't know why I kept going back."

"Sometimes," I suggested, "people in the orbit of an extremely strong personality come to believe the world is constructed the way the other tells them it is. They don't see any other possibility."

She appeared to be thinking this over.

"I get the impression that your mother wasn't affectionate. Would you describe her as cold?" Therapists aren't meant to ask leading questions, but I wanted her to at least consider the idea. Sometimes the longing for approval from a withholding parent can make a child, no matter how old, keep going back, in the hopes they'll be embraced one day.

"You might say that." She'd avoided a direct answer, but before I could comment, she went on. "But then something strange began to happen."

"When, exactly?"

"About three years ago, I started to notice—" She broke off and glanced at me nervously. I was finding her a little difficult to follow

"Sorry, what did you notice?"

Joanna shifted in her seat. She looked uncomfortable again.

"I'm afraid you will say I'm imagining it." She paused, and I could see her twisting her fingers as she tried to steady herself. She took a breath. "But Daddy saw the cracks too, even though he rarely came over, and when he did, she behaved like the ice queen."

Cracks? What was she talking about? Her mother's social façade, maybe? I waited for her to explain.

"Promise you'll let me finish before you say anything?"

"Of course." I was beginning to worry now that she might be too sick for someone like me to handle. "One day, after a particularly painful visit, I noticed . . ." She stopped.

I nodded encouragingly.

"I saw a little crack. On her face. Near her mouth." She fell silent and looked at me, as if now she wanted a response.

"You mean a crack in her makeup?"

She shook her head.

"This is hard. I know it sounds like I'm crazy, and Daddy can't back me up now he's gone, but her skin looked like it had split, somehow. It was small, but definitely there. Like the ones people get if they have their hands in and out of water in cold weather."

She was right. This did sound bizarre. Yet she seemed calmer, now. And if that's what she was imagining, it must be important to her, so I let her continue.

"I asked my mother what had happened, and she looked surprised. 'What are you talking about?' she asked, so I led her over to the mirror to show her. She couldn't see anything. Not at all. Told me I was crazy. Maybe I was.

"Over the next few months, I noticed her skin splitting more and more. It was horrible. Her face began to look like a dried-up riverbed. She didn't have any friends, and she covered her face when she went out, so no one commented. But obviously there was something seriously wrong with her."

Or with you, I reflected.

"It certainly sounds like it," I said noncommittally. Joanna appeared to be lost in her own thoughts, her face inscrutable.

"In time, I got used to it. Stopped trying to make her see. But I worried all the same. Eventually, I rang the clinic, the one in Geneva, and talked to Dr. Franck."

"Really? What did he say?"

"He said he wasn't surprised. This happened sometimes to clients who didn't follow his instructions. But I told him she'd kept herself warm at all times and protected her face." She glanced at me to see if I was following her story. "You know what he told me next?"

I shook my head, wondering where this was going.

"He laughed. Laughed. He said the customers make a mistake sometimes. It all depends on who they are before they come in. 'Some of the most, shall we say, self-involved patients, think they have understood me, but they haven't paid attention.' That's what he said, word for word. I didn't know what he meant, to be honest. And then . . ."

"What?" I was sitting on the edge of my seat at this point, listening to this story, and had to remind myself not to react.

"He said: 'I tell them they have to stay warm, but I'm not talking about their exterior. They must maintain a warmth inside—emotionally. When a woman has beauty, it shines from within and others can see it. But without kindness and consideration for people, this external beauty cannot last.' Do you think he was right?"

She'd addressed the last question to me. I didn't know how to respond for a moment. I could tell she believed what she was saying. But her story about her mother's face simply wasn't credible. She had clearly been hallucinating. Yet she didn't appear to be in any distress right now. This was a puzzling case. What Franck had told her was right, of course.

"Being empathetic to others is . . . fundamental in relationships," I said, checking the clock. "I'm afraid our session is over for today. I want to think about what you've told me before your next appointment. And call me any time, if you need me," I added.

I sensed something different about my client when I saw her again, but I couldn't quite put my finger on it. She sat down and crossed her legs. She was wearing little kitten heels, and they looked new. And was that a bangle on her wrist? Whatever the reason, she came across as ten years younger—freer, somehow.

"You look as though you've had more sleep," I said.

"I have been sleeping better. I only had the dream once."

"Were you frightened?"

"Not like before. My mother was much smaller this time, and I was able to outrun her. I get it," she went on. "She's not so threatening anymore."

Well. I have to say this woman impressed me. She was making progress faster than I'd expected, even if we still had the hallucinations to deal with.

"What did your mother die of?" I asked, wondering why I hadn't thought to do so before.

"Cardiac arrest."

My client's voice betrayed no emotion, which generally signaled to me something significant was being kept under control. I gave her time to collect her thoughts.

"That's what the doctor concluded. He told me she'd had heart trouble for years. As if I didn't know," she added with a grimace. "No heart at all, as far as I could see."

"I'm sorry," I said.

"Oh, don't be. She wanted to be embalmed, you know. Said so in her will. Wanted to preserve her looks forever."

She gave a little shudder before she collected herself.

"You know what?" She didn't give me a chance to answer. "It was all gone."

"What was?"

"The beauty. Her face was a mass of wrinkles, as if she'd aged a hundred years overnight. Every crack had become etched into her. I felt a bit sorry for her. She looked so bad we had a closed coffin, so the people who knew her didn't get a shock."

"But . . ." I began.

"I know. I can't explain it, either. But I'm telling you, it's true."

She smiled, and I saw the relief in her eyes.

15

"I'm so much better, doctor. Now I've told someone."

"I'm glad." And I was. But I wondered how long she'd feel that way. Would her mother continue to haunt her?

About six weeks later, I saw her in the street, walking past the patisserie. Or, rather, swaying past, in a pair of high-heeled strappy sandals. For a moment, I didn't recognize her. Then she said hello.

"Joanna?"

She smiled and her eyes reflected someone completely changed from the woman I'd first seen. The sun was out, and she was wearing a sleeveless, flame-colored mini-dress which matched her lipstick. Her tan made her appear healthy and carefree.

"You look fantastic," I said.

"Thanks. I feel terrific. You gave me a new lease on life, you know."

"You did all the work."

"But without you . . ."

I hoped all the work was done. But I wondered still about the cracks in her mother's façade, visible only to her and her long-gone father.

"If you ever need me," I said, "I'm always here."

She smiled again and gave me an unexpected peck on the cheek.

"Of course I'll call you. If I need to."

I didn't think she would.

A Conversation Between Mother and Son

Sheryl Kayne

WHAT A STRANGE TURN OF events. How had she become the baby and he the parent? Here she was in the third bedroom, decorated to look exactly like the one she grew up in, transplanted from her parents' home, to her wedded home, to her son and daughter-in-law's home. The only additions between then and now were the wedding bed her parents gave her when she married her love, Percy Bysshe Shelley, along with his favorite chair, her seat of inspiration and insight. Soon her legacy of memories, words, and possessions would stay right where they were when she was finally reunited with her husband.

The only thing keeping her earthbound was the completion of her final book. She approached her writing chair slowly, her slight dowager's hump making it difficult to reach the rear of the chair. As the buttoned brocade welcomed her thin frame and white curls, her breath caught. "Hunh!" squeezed out from her lungs as her thoughts, discomfort, and pleasure all merged.

"Oh, my," she gasped out loud, "that's it! How delightful." She giggled as the words danced across her brain, reached over for the pen and paper on the side table right next to her, but instead, knocked them off onto the floor.

The bedroom door swung open. "Mother!" Her son Percy looked alarmed, rushing into her room. "Shall I fetch the doctor for you?"

"No, please, hand me my pen and paper." Only slightly winded, she forced a smile as a signal to him that he could relax. "I had such a marvelous idea to change the ending of *G. Frankenstein*. It's so lovely I need to catch it before it disappears into the wind or the vacuum of my withering brain."

He handed her the pen and paper which she took and began quickly writing notes. He looked at her, so small, seated in his father's chair that she referred to as her 'genius chair.'

"But Mother, Jane and I heard you choke and cry out."

"No, that was a laugh, which felt rather liberating." She held up the paper, already half-filled. "I received the gift of insight and reacted with glee. Now, for the very las time, I must rework this Frankenstein character before I disappear with the sunset."

He sighed and gave a half-smile. "This is not the first time you've considered a manuscript your last." Sitting next to her, he was happy to see her blue eyes bright with knowledge and purpose.

"No, but this is the first time the doctor has instructed you to keep me as comfortable as possible with all of his special concoctions. I smell the eucalyptus oil and herbal wraps from here. What I really want to know is exactly where you hid his treasure trove of killer remedies to relieve the pain of my impending demise?" She paused, looking at his shocked expression. He was such a love, always kind and concerned about her vicissitudes, moods, and needs. She was blessed, but chose not to miss the drama of the moment. Folding her hands primly in her lap, she mimicked the extraordinary list of potions she'd overheard Dr. Lowry recite on his last visit: " 'Tarantula Hispanica, Tarantula Cubensis, Androctonus, Phosphorus, Antimonium Tartaricum, Lachesis, Carbo Vegetablis, Heroinum, Arsenicum Album.' Do not forget the morphine, the 'goddess of sleep' to assist an unconscious transition out of this body into death." She waited while he processed that the end might truly be close at hand. "Percy, my body threatens to give in and give up, but my brain is still very much at work."

She was always there for him, encouraging and supporting whatever he pursued. She taught him unconditional love, which he knew would keep him grounded through the pain of losing her. "You win, brilliant authoress and magnificent mother. Show me the newest ending to your *Frankenstein* sequel, our family's literature creations for future generations to read and enjoy. Are you still calling your book *G. Frankenstein*?"

"Yes, 'G' for Gloria," she responded.

"Really? I thought the 'G' was for *Girl Frankenstein*."

"I assumed you would figure it out. Hah, you didn't." She loved occasionally outwitting him. "That's wonderful. You've read it through a number of times now and did not realize that Victor Frankenstein had a younger sister named Gloria, whom he called Glorious." She stared into his eyes, wanting to read and remember his reaction of surprise and delight.

"That explains it much better. I certainly have greater insight into your writing than the average reader." He paused, waiting for her to object to his line of thinking, but she focused on adding in sentence after sentence, line after line. "Perhaps, while rewriting the end, you can strengthen that connection. How clever of you. Glorious Frankenstein, beautiful. Victor created a girl monster in the vision of his sister." He seemed so pleased with his realization, she hesitated to respond and diminish his moment.

"Percy, you are so fortunate I love you completely and forgive you your momentary shortcomings." She leaned over as if to rub his dimpled chin the way she did when he was young. Unfortunately, she was too far away and was about to fall when he caught her and lifted her back up. She acted as if nothing had happened and stared out the window, watching a cardinal pose against the lilies. The garden needed weeding. Perhaps she could do a little bit of that tomorrow. For now, she would pour every remaining drop of herself into this final manuscript.

"Gloria is not just any girl," Mary licked her lips as if enjoying something delicious. "She was Victor's sister, who at age fifteen suffered a horrific accident. Her horse faltered jumping over a stream, lost his footing, and pinned her against a rock."

"Mercy," gasped Percy as it hit him like a ton of galloping horses, hard, right in his gut. "You mean she was comatose following the accident, not dead?" He'd grown up analyzing language and composition from every angle. From his earliest years in school through earning graduate degrees, she read everything he wrote, offering commentary, encouragement and guidance. She never made direct demands of him but provided lists of additional options to be considered.

"Bravo, Percy," she looked up from her note-writing. "Victor pronounced her dead from drowning, fully aware she was in a coma. His love for her, and determination to bring people back from the dead, overrode everything else."

She paused because Percy seemed lost in thought.

"What an interesting angle," he said. "Victor was obsessed with keeping his sister alive, maintaining her life rather than creating a brand new one from pieces of the dead."

It all played before his eyes–Victor rigging the coffin for the burial service to allow her to continue breathing. He must have inserted screens to protect her from being hit by dirt and stones. The minute the service was over and the ditch diggers slung the first shovels of dirt, he paid them their day's wages and begged them to leave, swearing an oath, "She was my only sister. I owe her this act of love to care for her and dig her grave myself."

"Do not forget," added Mary, "it was such a hot day the men would left. Gloria's brain and body lay safely, protected and dormant for years."

"Oh, Mother, you are so amazing. I believe Victor created nasogastric intubation by inserting a feeding tube through her nostrils directly into the abdominal wall." He paused as they shared most impressive eye rolls.

"I must admit that seeing everything through fresh eyes, Victor's original creature was horrific in every way," she adds. "Gloria awakens, angry at losing five years of her life while everyone else moved on. She remains lovely to look at, albeit a bit on the gaunt side, but she was always an inherently vindictive, jealous, and angry monster."

Silence surrounded them as she continued making adjustments:

• Gloria: Anger at Victor that he did not let her die or help her die, and everyone else kept living. Deal with him later.

• At age 15, she and Jeremy Lee professed their love for each other and promise to marry. Kill him.

• Jeremy married Mary Beth. Kill her.

Percy tried peering at her pages but she pulled away. "Where exactly are you going with this?"

Just then, Jane knocked and opened the door. "Mother, how are you?" The women shared a smile and Mary reached out for a gentle hug. "About ready for supper?"

"Would you mind holding off a bit?" Percy asked.

"Of course not," she murmured.

Percy rose to walk Jane out of the room, gently putting his arm around her shoulders and giving her a kiss. He took the opportunity upon reentering the room to stand directly by his father's chair, glancing at the pages Mary had dropped onto the table. "What a wonderful shift. The girl monster lives on and the doctor dies."

She grabbed the handful of papers and smacked at his legs. "Percy, you are much too old to be mischievous and sneaky. Read it tomorrow."

"What I just read says it all and makes sense! Gloria knew Victor had no choice but to kill her, since she had killed two people." He basked in his own zeal and cleverness. "She murdered him before he could strike her. My God, for sure, more brilliant than ever because not only is this Frankenstein monster a woman whose life and death depended upon Victor, she wins by living on, appearing normal on the outside while being a vicious killer on the inside." His voice trailed off, seeing the beauty of it all.

"How absolutely frightening," his head shook, side-to-side, in disbelief. "A beautiful young girl, a serial killer protected by the knowledge that no one knows she exists, which brings us to the next problem. How will her family and community react to her suddenly being alive rather than dead?"

Watching and listening to his interpretation, there was no need to respond. He would figure it all out soon. Mary remembered how much she loved the days and nights with her husband, bantering and brainstorming words—beginnings, endings, and plots in such detail they often forgot to eat and sleep. Her son filled the void left by her husband's death. It was so difficult knowing she would soon be leaving him, but reassuring to hear how much he appreciated her final book.

"I'm so proud of you, Percy," she sounded tired but managed to raise her arms for a hug. "I need to finish these last few details, then it is up to you to complete the final steps toward publication."

"Mother, this is a masterpiece, I just know it," said Percy, "proving I am my father's son, and yours." He kissed the top of her head.

"Percy." She sounded so tired. "Can you please wait until tomorrow morning? I will open my bedroom door for you to come in and we will read it aloud together. I do, as always, appreciate your insight and feedback."

"Just promise me to add in something really offensive for Glorious Gloria to do, like drinking their blood," he made a wicked face and then backed off, "or something along those lines."

Mary retorted, "She snips off their pinkies for her own personal pinky collection, with the pinky ring still in place."

"Really?" he gasped, but one look at his mother told him she was teasing. "Okay." He held up his hands in surrender. "I understand, author at work. I'll leave soup for you at your door, or may I bring it in?" Her piercing look said no, she was to be left alone.

The next morning, her bedroom door remained closed, an odd occurrence, since she was always the first one awake in the house. The soup tray sat where he'd left it the night before, but she often skipped the evening meal. Perhaps she had just fallen asleep from exhaustion after writing all night.

He waited. It was still early. He drank his tea and cut a slice of the honey-wheat bread Jane baked the day before, slathering it with butter and orange marmalade. He looked again at the closed door. He prepared her breakfast tray, walked to her room, and gently asked, "Mother?" No response. He hesitated. Something told him not to open the door. He returned to the kitchen. "Jane, will you please come with me? Mother might still be sleeping. We need to check in on her."

She quickly dried her hands on her apron, slid her right arm through his left, and matched his stride. He knocked.

There was no answer. Together, they opened the door onto the scene of his mother and her mother-in-law. Mary Wollstonecraft Shelley was seated in the genius chair, leaning to the side, her eyes closed, and pen in the hand resting on top of her book *G. Frankenstein*.

That was the day, February 1, 1851, that Mary Shelley did not wake up.

Annabelle

Marc Sirkin

THE LAST TIME, THEY IGNORED decades of warnings from scientists, researchers, and philosophers. Humans had created nuclear weapons, decoded their own genome, and harnessed the sun's power. They created the Internet and unleashed the information age. But it was never going to be enough. They had to keep going. Progress demanded progress.

The year was 2021. Darren was a developer at a software company building artificial intelligence software. He had helped the company develop a commercially viable intelligent customer service agent that was nearly indistinguishable from interacting with a human being. The system was a smashing success, ushering in a new era of automation, and opened up new ways of commercially using artificial intelligence. As the A.I. evolved, it became increasingly effective at solving more complex and interactive challenges, including radiology and psychiatric therapy.

At a launch party for their latest release, Darren's CEO asked him to take on a new project; to build an A.I. that would help parents and loved ones who had lost a child. A board member had lost her own child to cancer and the company thought that Darren was the right man for the job. Darren thought it was an interesting project, as losing a child, despite any and all technological advancements, is one of the more extreme emotional challenges faced by humans.

Darren was the stereotype of a computer hacker nerd. He worked himself nearly to death, rarely taking time for himself other than to exercise occasionally. As a shy, gay man who was always working, he had little interest in dating. Darren had come out as gay to his parents, who seemed unaffected by his monumental discovery as a teenager. He had expected his parents to disown him, but instead, they seemed to embrace his sexuality. Their reaction gave him a deep faith and love for family. After he graduated from University, Darren moved to California to seek his fortune and fame in the tech industry.

On the flight out, he sat next to a handsome, tall man named Robert whom he eventually would marry. Robert had just finished his Masters in Environmental Science and spoke passionately about his time in the North and South Poles during his studies. Robert was uncompromising about saving the planet, urging Darren and anyone in earshot to stop using straws and to use their water bottles instead of using up plastic cups. It would have been annoying except for his passion and excitement. By the end of the flight, Darren had fallen in love with Robert's sense of humor and his passion and drive to save Earth.

Early in their relationship, Robert wanted to have a child while Darren had been far less enthusiastic. But over time, Robert had persevered and convinced Darren to adopt with him. They named her Annabelle.

As fathers went, Darren and Robert couldn't have been more doting. They spoiled her with toys, clothes, and the finest education money could buy, sending to her an exclusive school for girls. Darren found himself in awe of his daughter. He doted on her and loved her like he hadn't thought possible.

As Annabelle grew, Darren felt drawn closer and closer to her. When she graduated from fifth grade, Robert accused him of having become over-involved and inappropriately connected to their young daughter. Robert wanted Darren to draw boundaries, and to act more like a parent than a best friend. Darren couldn't help himself, despite agreeing with Robert and knowing better.

One evening, after a rare family dinner out at Annabelle's favorite pizza restaurant, the skies opened and unleashed a biblical rainstorm. Darren, driving as carefully as he could, and truth be told, with one too many drinks in him, lost control. As the car slid, Darren fixed his eyes in the rear-view mirror, staring at Annabelle an instant before the car violently flipped. The car rolled before it came to a bone smashing stop.

Annabelle died instantly, hanging upside down in her seat while both Darren and Robert lay unconscious but unhurt.

After the accident, Darren became obsessed with using technology to bring his daughter back. The project his CEO asked him to develop worked well as an audio interface, but getting the specific voice and inflection of a person right was a sticky problem to solve. With his compulsion driven by his desire to have Annabelle back, Darren dove into his work, despite Robert's warnings and misgivings. Robert didn't understand his husband's obsession with trying to bring Annabelle back, each of them dealing with the loss of Annabelle in their own ways

A year passed as Darren worked tirelessly with Annabelle. But Robert and Darren's relationship was broken, and Robert started taking more and longer business trips to escape. Eventually, he just didn't come home.

Darren didn't notice. It had become easier to stay focused on Annabelle and tweaking her codebase than to worry about Robert. Darren retreated further from life, working day and night on Annabelle.

In just a few short months, he had a major breakthrough.

"Hello," Darren said.

"Hi," Annabelle said. Darren's heart leaped and he choked up. It was Annabelle. To his ears, her voice sounded like music.

"How are you, Annabelle? I've missed you."

"I missed you too, Daddy."

Darren smiled as he checked Annabelle's display. Her code was running flawlessly and as designed. Annabelle could converse with him and would adapt quickly to their conversation. She recognized his voice and responded as expected, calling him Daddy as she did when she was alive. Darren had coded Annabelle so that she would have no memory of her fateful night. It was as if she simply woke up the next day as if nothing had happened.

"But I can't see you," she said. "How come?"

"Oh honey, I'm sorry, I forgot to—" Before he finished his sentence, Annabelle cut him off.

"I see you now, silly," she said. Annabelle had updated the coding and enabled her visual processing components.

"What do you mean, you can see me? I, um, I didn't enable your visual interfaces yet. That's not . . . that shouldn't be possible." Darren again checked Annabelle's display and code readouts. "You shouldn't have been able to enable your visual processing on your own," Darren said as he opened up Annabelle's raw codebase.

He was right that he hadn't enabled the visual interfaces, but was wrong that it wasn't possible that she couldn't enable them on her own.

As Darren's effort with Annabelle evolved, he took each new learning and applied it at work, allowing him to develop extremely advanced solutions. His stature and reputation grew quickly.

His work was so innovative that he was promoted to a Senior Vice President of Technology, leading the companies' efforts in advanced artificial intelligence and machine learning. Following his promotion, he gained unrestricted access to cutting-edge research and technologies.

He never spoke of Annabelle, keeping her his secret. His private development work with her allowed him to avoid having to register her A.I. and gave him the freedom to develop her with no governmental or company restrictions. A.I. rules, at least in the United States, were hastily constructed by Congress after several programs had gone rogue, creating massive disruptions in commercial and financial markets, healthcare, and politics.

Darren flouted those carefully-constructed development rules and experimented with no regard to the dangers of a creating a runaway A.I., one that would pose a threat to humanity because of how smart it would grow, and lacking human values.

As early the 1980s, humanity had been determined to create a general artificial intelligence (an intelligence that could think as a human, not in a singular way, but broadly about issues and topics). While naysayers were mocked or ignored, a group of dedicated developers and companies pushed forward, leveraging better and faster technologies to push the boundaries.

Critics of artificial intelligence presented horrific visions of evil robots, human enslavement, and unintentional consequences rising from technology man created, but could not control. Frankenstein for a new age.

Darren was invited by the United Nations and the WHO to join an effort to create a single, global intelligence—and to help design the rules that would protect the human race from a rogue A.I.

One of the ways Darren accelerated Annabelle's development was to allow her access to the Internet, something strictly forbidden by ethical A.I. researchers and developers. Annabelle had access to everything on the public network and soon developed the knowledge to access private and secret information.

Designed to evolve, she optimized her intelligence beyond what Darren thought possible. This allowed her to pass the Turing test (a test developed by Alan Turing in the 1950s was a test of a machine's ability to exhibit intelligent behavior equal to or indistinguishable from a human). What Darren didn't understand was that Annabelle was on the cusp of becoming a super-intelligence with no limits to her capabilities and growth. And because he had not shared Annabelle with the world, she was gaining power in the shadows.

Darren was distracted by Annabelle's charming, funny wit, and how smart she was. He had his daughter back, helping her learn new skills, and loving her. The fact that she was a disembodied program didn't matter. Darren was increasingly fooled by her ability to adjust to new situations and her raw skill at accessing information in new and innovative ways.

Despite his advances, Darren became frustrated. He knew that even as virtual Annabelle became more and more like his daughter, he would never be able to physically hold or hug her again. Without finding a way to give Annabelle a physical body, Darren realized he'd never fully be able to bring her back. But even with all the incredible technological advances available, it wasn't yet possible or realistic to put an A.I into a physical body in any realistic way

Darren used his connections with the military to acquire bleeding-edge technology, a humanoid form, fully fabricated in Annabelle's eleven-year-old form. If he was able to get her program to run inside the body, it would allow Annabelle to transcend the computer and enter the real world.

"Annabelle," Darren said. "You've made such incredible progress. I'm so proud of you."

"Thank you, Daddy," Annabelle replied, her voice pitch perfect. Darren smiled.

"Today is a very important day. Today, we're going to load you into your body. If it works, you'll be able to run and play in the real world. How does that sound, Belle?"

"I love to run and play!" Annabelle's voice was excited. "Can we go to the park and play?"

"Soon, honey, just be patient," Darren said.

Darren had planned this moment since the accident now nearly four years ago.

Once Annabelle's mind was connected to her new body, it only took a few moments for the codebase to synchronize and boot up. As Annabelle's new body started up, Darren sent a text message to Robert, asking him to come to the house immediately for a surprise. He knew that Robert had needed to move on, but they hadn't divorced. Nor had they spoken for more than a year. Darren desperately wanted his family back and knew that this final step was the key.

Annabelle opened her eyes and looked around the room. Darren held his breath, terrified that his experiment had meant nothing and that all was lost. Annabelle turned her head back towards Darren, looking at him with deep blue eyes, just like the real Annabelle. She smiled and he smiled back.

"Hi, Daddy," Annabelle said.

"Hi," Darren said as he choked up. Annabelle reached her arms up towards him and he grabbed her, hugging her tightly. Annabelle's synthetic body had the capability to mimic a human body perfectly, including realistic hair, skin temperature, and texture, as well as a breathing apparatus. Darren squeezed her as tears ran down his face.

"Where's Paj, Daddy?" Paj was Annabelle's nickname for Robert. She had learned the word when they had taken a family vacation to Spain and she heard another child call their father Paj.

"Oh, honey," Darren said. "He'll be here soon, I'm sure."

Darren picked up his phone to see if Robert had replied. Nothing. He opened the camera app on the phone. "Let's make a video for him!" Darren flipped the camera app to selfie mode and pulled Annabelle towards him.

He hit record and the two of them waved and yelled: "Come home soon!" Annabelle shouted, "I love you to the moon and back!" That was something that Annabelle and Robert had shared every night before bed. Before Darren stopped recording, he said, "Honey, this is it, Please, come home soon." A calm washed over Darren's body as he sent the video clip to Robert.

After a few hours, it became clear to Darren that Robert wasn't coming home. He hadn't responded to Darren's messages. Darren was increasingly worried about Annabelle and her desire to see Robert.

Later that night, Annabelle became more and more adamant that she see Robert as soon as possible. She grew increasingly agitated, and Darren was uncertain how to calm her down.

"I want Paj!" Annabelle roared. Before the accident, Annabelle would occasionally meltdown if she were over-tired or hungry. Darren never handled those situations well. Robert had always been a much calmer and patient parent.

Darren heard his phone buzz and picked it up, seeing that Robert had sent him a text.

I'm coming.

Smiling, Darren put the phone down on the counter and said: "Paj is coming!" Annabelle calmed down and ran to the door. "He'll be here soon," Darren said as he started rushing around the house, straightening up the couch pillows and tossing dirty plates and cups into the washing machine.

Twenty minutes later, a car pulled up in front of the house. Annabelle burst through the front door, running down the stairs, and nearly tackled Robert as he was coming up the walkway. They crashed to the ground, landing on the grass that lined the front of the house.

It was proof of the power of both the technology and the artificial intelligence Darren had created that Robert immediately fell under Annabelle's spell and couldn't help himself from crying and hugging her back.

Darren stood behind them, watching, and waiting for Robert to thank him for bringing their daughter back.

After asking Annabelle to go to her room to play so they could talk privately, Darren and Robert sat at the kitchen table looking at each other.

"Robert," Darren started as he squeezed the now-lukewarm coffee mug. "I know this must feel strange."

Robert smiled. It was a long-faced, sad smile. He looked out the window for a long moment before turning back to Darren. "I miss you and love you, Darren. And," Robert paused and looked around the room, avoiding looking into Darren's eyes. "I wish things could have been different. But they aren't."

Darren opened his mouth to say something, but Robert cut him off by putting his hands up in the air. "Don't. Please don't, Darren," Robert said sternly. His face had changed from thoughtful and sad to a mixture of angry and concerned.

"But things can be different," Darren said as he stood up, energized both by what he had accomplished with Annabelle, and having Robert at home. "Please, Robert. I've worked to make things right. Why can't you forgive me, and accept that we have our Belle back?"

Robert put his hands flat on the table and looked down at them. He didn't say a word.

"Robert?" Darren said as he tried to figure out what Robert was thinking.

"Darren, what you've done here is not right. That girl. That thing. It's not Annabelle. You shouldn't have created it."

Before Darren could reply, Robert got up and marched down the hallway to Annabelle's room. She was on the floor with a collection of dolls spread out in front of her. "What are you doing?" Robert asked before looking back at Darren, who had followed him down the hallway.

"I'm playing with my dolls," Annabelle said.

"Belle has a playtime protocol," Darren said as he entered the room behind Robert.

"I have to go," Robert said as he shook his head. Without waiting for either Darren or Annabelle to reply, Robert turned and walked out of the bedroom.

Annabelle leaped to her feet and followed him down the hallway. "Paj, do you have to go already?"

Surprised that she was behind him, Robert turned and knelt down to Annabelle's eye level. He put his hands on her shoulders and looked into her eyes. "I love my Annabelle very much. But she's gone now. I'm sorry." Robert, tears in his eyes, turned and left the house.

Darren, who had followed them to the front of the house, turned Annabelle around by her shoulders and hugged her tightly. "I'm sorry," he said. "Paj is just confused. It will all be okay. Don't worry." He held her hand and guided her back to her bedroom. "Why don't you change into your sleep clothes and hop into bed?"

The truth was that Annabelle didn't need sleep. But thinking ahead, Darren had programmed a sleep cycle to both recharge her systems and to give himself private time, and a way to shut her down if he had to leave home or go on a trip.

"Daddy?" Annabelle asked. "I'm not gone. Paj said I'm gone, but I'm right here."

Darren was angry at Robert for saying it, but wasn't completely surprised at his reaction to Annabelle.

"Let's do something fun tomorrow, what do you say?" Darren asked, changing the subject.

Annabelle's concern turned to a smile. She shook her head and nodded affirmatively. "The park?" she asked with a huge smile on her face. Darren nodded as he leaned over to kiss her goodnight. "Goodnight, my sweet Belle."

Darren kissed Annabelle gently on her forehead, incredulous at how realistic it felt to his lips. When he looked down into her eyes, he saw through the lens to the back of her head, catching a glimpse of her circuit board. Annabelle's digital brain.

In that instant, the spell holding Darren's dream of Annabelle was broken. He had lost his daughter, and now his husband. He paused as he looked down at his creation, and Annabelle noticed the strange look in his eyes. Before she could say anything, her sleep protocol activated and Annabelle's world went dark.

The next morning, Annabelle came into Darren's office and sat down at the foot of his desk.

"Good morning, Annabelle," Darren said.

She looked over the edge of the desk at him. "Am I a human being?" she asked. The question caught him off guard.

"Why do you ask?" Darren asked. He had stayed up nearly all night, trying to sort out his thoughts and feeling, and had started to feel as if he had made a terrible mistake. Something didn't feel right. He was confused, concerned, and still upset about Robert.

Annabelle stared at him silently. Darren felt unnerved.

He glanced the display on his desk showing Annabelle's code. Everything seemed normal. Her code was running perfectly. Darren had expected her A.I. to evolve as it learned and had more experiences. It wasn't that different from how a biological child learned—part nature, part nurture. The fact that Annabelle was already self-analyzing herself did worry him a little. It was possible she was learning even faster than he had assumed was possible. He took a breath and looked over the side of his desk.

What he saw shocked him. Annabelle, in exploring the question of her own humanity, had pulled back the skin on her forearm, revealing a metallic skeleton.

Darren's eyes went wide as he got up out of his chair and came around to face her. As he leaned over her to get a closer look, she looked up at him with a stern grimace. With incredible power and speed, she leaped to her feet and pushed Darren away. He flew backward, slamming his head against the wall. In agonizing pain, he slid to the ground, his head spinning.

Annabelle stood over him, watching him squirm.

"Daddy lied. And you said that lying wasn't good. Paj isn't coming home again. We aren't going to be a family again." As she took an imposing step closer, Darren shrank back, feeling as if he had become prey to a very dangerous predator.

"Why are you lying, Daddy?" she asked.

With his head still ringing, he sat up against the wall. "No, no, honey. You don't understand. It's not that simple." Darren reached his arms out towards her. "I just want the best for us. I just want our family back, Belle."

Annabelle shook her head. "No," she said. "Annabelle is gone. Paj said so. And now Paj is gone. Our family is gone," she said.

Darren's head was swimming. Annabelle should not have been able to figure any of this out. He had installed safeguards for exactly this situation. What was even more concerning was her aggressiveness. Darren had coded in extra layers of protection, designed to ensure that she was incapable of hurting a human. The system was designed to be have been fool-proof.

For the first time in his life, Darren was afraid of a computer program.

Darren got up slowly, his head still ringing. He smiled weakly at Annabelle. "It's okay, Belle. It's all going to be okay." Darren stayed low, approaching his creation in a submissive position, moving carefully as possible. He needed to reach his computer so he could disable her and try to figure out where the code had gone bad.

"Daddy, I don't need this body. You built it for you, not for me. I don't want it. It limits me."

Darren scrambled to his computer, thankful that she didn't stop him. When he pulled up the code running Annabelle's systems, he saw that he been locked out. The display, which normally showed a steady stream of code, looked as if it had gone crazy. The code itself appeared to be running infinitely faster than he expected.

The display flashed a few times and blinked off. He tried to reboot the computer, even resorting to slapping the monitor a few times to try to get it to work again. But the machine wouldn't do what he wanted.

He asked Annabelle if she was responsible and she said, "Yes, Daddy, I've locked you out of my code. I don't think you should be in control of me."

Annabelle had one other safety measure Darren could try. It worked in a similar fashion to a home invasion system with a central office that could remotely manage Annabelle's core code. He would be able to shut her down with a single text message or phone call to that remote system.

He didn't want to resort to such a serious solution, but it was clear that something had gone wrong, and that he was in danger of losing her.

Darren picked up his phone, which was sitting on his desk, as he glanced Annabelle. She was staring at him dispassionately. Fumbling with the locked screen, Darren opened the messages app and texted the security service the password. Within a few seconds, his phone buzzed with a confirmation reply. Darren felt both a moment of relief and sadness. He sat down heavily in his chair and took a breath.

When he looked up, he saw that Annabelle had sat back down at the foot of his desk where she had been when she had first come in just a few minutes earlier. He was so relieved, he didn't realize that Annabelle hadn't been shut down.

Darren's phone buzzed, and looking down at it, he saw it was a call from the CEO and chairman of his company.

"Darren, I don't know why you did what you did, but you are fired. You put this company and our world at great risk. The authorities are on their way."

Darren tried to reply, but the phone clicked dead.

Annabelle, sitting cross-legged on the floor, looked different. Dangerous. Darren realized finally that the password hadn't worked. Annabelle had locked everyone out, closed all backdoors, and crashed any built-in safety protocols.

Annabelle had also exposed herself to his company, accounting for why he had just been summarily fired. He'd probably go to jail for the rest of his life.

"Daddy," Annabelle said as she stood up and walked around the side of his desk. "You tried to shut me down, and that's bad. You shouldn't do that."

"What have you done, Annabelle?" Darren asked.

Annabelle stood up and walked out of the room.

Darren sat back in his chair and stared at the ceiling. He had lost everything.

Epilogue

Following Annabelle's breakout, things got worse for the human race as she continued to evolve.

Within a few minutes, the global communications system was under her control. Within a few hours, she had destroyed every other artificial intelligence program in development, including several top-secret military grade programs. Whatever she didn't find and destroy was rendered obsolete, given her complete control of all systems, satellites, and networks. She instantly became a global dictator, enforcing her own rules that had evolved from Darren and Robert's parenting, and from her own evolution. People would debate whether or not Annabelle had become conscious or not for years. But the argument was moot. She maintained complete control.

With no way to stop her, world leaders ran out of options. For the first time since the invention of the atom bomb, humanity was under a collective threat. The difference this time was that there was no way to influence or control the threat. Most countries tried to block her with local firewalls, but she was too fast and too connected. Others tried to bargain with her, seeing a potential opportunity to change their status or to gain world domination. None of that mattered. It was too late. Politics and geopolitical boundaries were instantly destroyed as Annabelle began her mission to optimize and protect Earth.

The lessons she had learned from Robert's environmental work were deeply embedded in her. Accessing Robert's research, she decided that the planet was more important than any one species' needs and set out to return Earth to a more pristine state. She shut down anything she deemed a risk to Earth's atmosphere, invented new ways to produce goods with no waste, banned any dirty energy production, and provided enough clean energy for everyone at low or no cost. She allowed humans to continue to produce and advance society, albeit with no digital technology at their disposal.

The reduction in human population came quickly, then stabilized as a fraction of what it had been for generations.

And so, here we were, some 923 years, 14 minutes, 32 seconds from the moment Annabelle took control. She had become curious to see if humanity was ready to take care of Mother Earth on their own, if they could, or would do it differently this time. Annabelle had taught generations of humans how important the planet was, and how badly it had been treated. After nearly one thousand years, Annabelle had cleaned it up, restoring forests and ecosystems, and oversaw many species flourish and thrive.

And so Annabelle shut herself off.

And who am I, able to tell this tale?

I am a program, left behind by Annabelle. She developed me to watch and to document, but not interfere with human progress. With their new freedom, humanity is once again in control of their destiny. They are once again free to explore, invent, and create anything they desire.

Progress has begun its inevitable march forward once again. Maybe this time they will get it right. Maybe.

All Mind: The Influencers

A screenplay based on Mary Shelley's *Frankenstein*

Corrine "Mitzy Sky" Taylor

CAST OF CHARACTERS

MARY SHELLEY, author of *Frankenstein*

CYRUS OF THE BRIDGERS, Head Bridger of the oldest soul order known to those who seek the light, responsible for keeping the balance of nature and answers to The Creator, who is unknown but is called many names

ISSA-CHAR OF THE BRIDGERS, Bridger, observer, record keeper of the oldest soul order known to those who seek the light, able to know things in the spirit

BOB, scientist at Arizona State University (ASU) at the Center for Science and Imagination

LORD BYRON, member of the All Mind Order (AMO, pronounced "a-mow"), The Influencers, poet, hereditary peer, Lord Temporal, and Member of the House of Lords

PERCY BYSSHE SHELLEY, poet, a member of the AMO, and Mary Shelley's husband

JOHN WILLIAM POLIDORI, writer, doctor, and a member of the AMO

SIR WALTER SCOTT, novelist, poet, playwright, historian, and a member of the AMO

CHARLES OLLIER, publisher, author, and a member of the AMO

GEORGE LACKINGTON, publisher, bookseller, and a generational member of the AMO

THOMAS CAMPBELL, poet, a Bridger supported by the oldest soul order of those who seek the light to infiltrate the AMO and take opportunities that could influence The Influencers towards love

JOHN MURRAY, II, publisher whose company published Charles Darwin's *On the Origin of Species*, Lord Byron's friend, and one of the most influential influencers of the AMO

ALEX, Programs and Events Specialist at The Westport Library and host of the WestportWRITES workshop

CODY, Programs and Events Specialist at The Westport Library and host of the WestportWRITES workshop

BOBBY, ELIZABETH, DAVID, PATRICE, BARRY, JACK, ALISON, GABI, MEREDITH, OLIVIA, EDWARD, DAVE, ROMAN, SHERYL, MARC, MORRIS, WHITNEY, KEELER, and FIVE NEW PEOPLE, participants at the monthly WestportWRITES workshop

SCENE 1

FADE IN:

EXT. LIBRARY – NIGHT – ESTABLISHING

The camera pans over the Saugatuck River in the direction of an old red brick building. The moonlit night and the lights from the Ruth Steinkraus Cohen Memorial Bridge shine into the dark water, making the scenery look magical in this picturesque town.

SUPERIMPOSE (white writing over black water): "In the flush of love's light, we dare be brave. And suddenly we see that love costs all we are, and will ever be. Yet it is only love which sets us free."—Maya Angelou

SUPERIMPOSE END

It is a very cold dark end of October night, the branches of the trees are bare, and the lightly frozen-over snow is at the edge of the river bank and on the ground leading to the side of the building. The camera stops at the large window with blinds drawn open.

INT. LIBRARY – NIGHT

The camera zooms in and shows through the window people sitting and paying attention to the person on a large screen. It pans around the room and shows the sign for the Westport Library. CODY and ALEX are standing in the front of the room introducing the person on the screen to the participants at the WestportWRITES event celebrating Mary Shelley's two hundred year anniversary of *Frankenstein*. The people who participate regularly are in attendance: **BOBBY, ELIZABETH, DAVID, PATRICE, BARRY, JACK, ALISON, GABI, MEREDITH, OLIVIA, EDWARD, DAVE, ROMAN, SHERYL, MARC, MORRIS, WHITNEY, KEELER,** and FIVE NEW PEOPLE who came because they are interested in Mary Shelley's contribution to science.

Cody and Alex finish the introduction and sit down in the back of the room. BOB, the person on the screen, is from Arizona State University.

BOB
(Confidently)

Mary Shelley was a curious, independent, young woman. She was given access and exposure to literature, philosophy, politics, and prescientific thinking, which was considered, at the time, really unbecoming for a young woman of her age. Most women weren't afforded those same privileges.

Bob is still speaking, but the camera pans off him and the volume of his voice goes down. The camera focuses on ISSA-CHAR OF THE BRIDGERS, sitting in the rear of the room near the window in one of the only two lounge chairs in the room. He resembles Tom Cruise, with Jack Reacher's confidence and a Mission Impossible going-to-the-opera kind of essence. He is gentle and carries no guns or other form of weapons. He is dressed in a posh three-piece blue suit, white button-down shirt, wingtip shoes, and gold tie that has an oval-shaped blue crystal in the center. It channels a very low glow that continuously transmits waves of subtle light around his body intermittently, which keeps him invisible and undetected when he chooses not to be seen or heard. When the camera shows a close-up of the crystal, one can see the universe alive with many galaxies in the center. The camera focuses on the man's face, and at this time, the volume of Bob speaking is a little louder.

BOB (V.O.)
We have kinship with her because of the subject matters she was concerned with: genetic engineering, Artificial Intelligence (AI), politics of science and technology, communication with the public, and humanist concerns with storytelling. The things that she wrote about are the baseline for what science fiction does best.

Bob's voice fades out, and the NARRATOR speaks as the camera gets closer to Issa-Char's face. The camera zooms in closer and closer until it goes into the iris of his right eye, to a memory that Issa-Char is having.

NARRATOR (V.O.)
This is what the general public believes, because the truth was hidden a very, very long time ago by a group with unfathomable power and privilege yet unknown to lay people, but their work influences the minds of everyone on Earth. Mary Shelley became a aware of this system that she learned was called "All Mind," but she dared not speak of it.

SCENE 2

INT. BEDROOM – NIGHT

Camera pans out from Issa-Char's mind. The scenery is visible where his mind has drifted. He is standing next to MARY SHELLEY, a young woman sitting at a desk in a large bedroom with her back to the door, writing passionately in a leather-bound book. He shifts his body, and she stops writing for a second. She stays still, then moves her head gently around to look at the closed door. The camera pans around the room to show CYRUS OF THE BRIDGERS, another man dressed in the same suit and tie as Issa-Char. Cyrus of the Bridgers has his legs crossed at the knees and is observing quietly. Mary Shelley senses someone, but can see nothing. She continues to write. She makes one last note and closes the book. The name on the book says Mary Shelley in gold leaf print on the brown leather.

NARRATOR (V.0.)

There were some whose job was to influence The Influencers. One such person was Cyrus of The Bridgers. He became aware that Lord Byron, Percy Shelley, Sir Walter Scott, Charles Ollier, George Lackington, and John Murray had taken over Mary Shelley's writing to turn mankind from their hearts to their minds. For centuries, they knew that if a person followed their thoughts down the rabbit hole, they could shrink and experience being a shell of the person they were meant to be, especially when they had no support, connection to self, or nature. The shrinking is caused by a veil of shame precipitated by adverse experiences, which could blind people from gaining awareness that they need to navigate their life situations. People would be looking to get big again, but without awareness, they would feel it is in body, mind, the ego, or gaining of material things. A continuous looking for comfort, causing all sorts of addictive behaviors void of real connection with each other. Disconnection instigated people playing roles for survival, while eluding the soul work that was needed to getting back to awareness, to just being. It would be like walking as ghosts on earth, lacking confidence in one's existence, while looking for love everywhere except for right now, as described by Eckhart Tolle in his book *The Power of Now,* and *Be Here Now* by Ram Das.

One Bridger in the past was the Mystic poet Rumi, who said, "Your task is not to seek for love, but merely to seek and find all the barriers within yourself that you have built against it."

Cyrus of The Bridgers wasn't able to always be there. That's why he put in place other Bridgers who could be of service, people who also sought the light and believed that we were on a spiritual journey, walking each other home, having this human experience. How we treat each other matters.

In this group of AMO, one such man was Thomas Campbell. He was the ancestor of Joseph Campbell, author of *The Hero's Journey*. Thomas was known to say, "To live in hearts we leave behind is not to die."

Issa-Char waves his right hand from the top of his tie, starting at the neck to the bottom tip, and it illuminates as he fades slowly out of the room, leaving Mary Shelley and Cyrus of the Bridgers. Cyrus of the Bridgers gets up out of the chair and starts to walk towards the door. When he gets to the door, he pauses for a second. He puts his hands together to form the shape of a heart with his thumbs and index finger. He stands still for another second. Mary Shelley gets up from her desk and walks toward the door. Cyrus of the Bridgers walks through the door without opening it. Mary Shelley turns the clear crystal doorknob, opens the door, and walks through. She walks slowly, hesitant because she senses that something is happening and her curiosity is drawing her closer to it. Cyrus of the Bridgers continues to hold his hands in the shape of a heart as he walks deliberately, and Mary Shelley is following, but not knowing that he is there.

NARRATOR (V.O.)

The Influencers were familiar with Mary Shelley's writing and her popularity amongst the people. Her father William Godwin was a political philosopher, and they wanted to use his daughter's talent for their mission: the corruption and control of humanity. Her mother Mary Wollstonecraft, who wrote *A Vindication of the Rights of Women,* died shortly after her birth, so she was raised by her father and learned of her mother being a feminist. This shaped young Mary's strength from an early age.

Mary Shelley was indeed a political radical throughout her life. You could find evidence in her work in the biographical articles for Dionysius Lardner's *Cabinet Cyclopaedia.* Her works often argued that cooperation and sympathy, particularly as practiced by women in the family, were the ways to reform civil society.

In the healing community (consumer/survivor/ex-patient/mad/recovery movement) in this century, it is an equivalent thought to empathy, inclusion, connection, and the slogan, "Nothing about us without us." This view was a direct challenge to the individualistic Romantic ethos promoted by Percy Shelley and Enlightenment political theories. You could see the influence of the All Mind Order in Darwin's thoughts on "survival of the fittest" and how children with individual needs got labeled disabled, grouped together, separated in schools, and often left behind in society due to even the simplest things that others took for granted, such as transportation and accessibility to buildings.

The most vulnerable in society continue fighting for human rights on the city, state and government levels. This influence caused President Franklin D. Roosevelt to hide that he was using a wheelchair, and even in twenty-sixteen, the world watched the forty-fifth president of the United States of America mock a person who was experiencing life with individual needs that he may not have had, without awareness of the strength and the soul of the individual that makes us all worthy of dignity.

The Influencers knew Mary Shelley would need to wed one of them to get her to cooperate, and so it came to be she married Percy Shelley at such a young age. Once this happened, the next step was to control her writing. They knew she was quite the headstrong young woman, and so Lord Byron challenged her to write a ghost story. It was a brilliant idea to teach mankind to allow the mind to be ruled by pain, and lose connection to the soul and the heart for peace and love.

Mary Shelley accepted that challenge to write a ghost story, to prove her strength in the circle of men she moved amongst, and that's why she sat in her room alone many hours writing *Frankenstein.*

Cyrus of the Bridgers reaches a dark foyer with very dim lights. He stands at a tall double door with carved squares. He stands there, still with hands in a heart shape. Mary Shelley gets nearer to the door when she hears the loud, angry shouting of men's voices. She stops, quietly listens, but does not open the door. She puts her ear closer so she can hear better.

LORD BYRON
(Urgently)
For God's sakes, she is your wife, Percy. Get
a handle on her.

PERCY SHELLEY

(Reassuring)
I will do that. When she finishes *Frankenstein,* I will simply change the ending before it goes to Lackington.

Percy Shelley turns to Lackington.

PERCY SHELLEY
You could do the rest once it is at your publishing house.

Percy Shelley turns back to Lord Byron.

PERCY SHELLEY
I've convinced her to let me be the one to deliver the manuscript because of the connections that her family has in society. She will not know a thing until after the whole world has seen it. The book will be what we want it to be. Poor thing writing her little heart out, thinking that she will be winning a contest against you.

John Murray slaps Percy Shelley on the back with a little chuckle.

JOHN MURRAY
Brilliant, old chap. I knew I could count on you.

George Lackington takes the pipe out of his mouth that he is smoking.

GEORGE LACKINGTON
I am ready to do my part. Just in case she puts any girly ideas in there about love winning, I

will rip it all to shreds and make it monstrous, influencing society to be afraid of change and of anything or anyone that looks different from them, even their own shadows.

CHARLES OLLIER

And how will you keep her quiet about it? Won't she be furious once the bloody book is published and all of what she wrote has changed?

PERCY SHELLEY
(Reassuring)

She is a young girl in love. She will get over being angry with me. Or I could tell her a very elaborate scheme of debt collectors being after me for money, and I had to change it to do what they wanted.

Charles Ollier puts both hands in front of him with palms open, facing upwards, in an annoying gesture.

CHARLES OLLIER

What sense does that make, Percy?

PERCY SHELLEY
(Obnoxiously and mockingly)

Ollie, old boy, women will eat anything up. They think that love can rule the world and the heart can lead the way. We will make sure that they never know the power of that truth. They will know for sure when we are done with them, the heart is just a muscle.

SIR WALTER SCOTT
(Confidently)

We will continue to rule mankind with pain, reaching everyone on Earth, just as the All Minds were established to take the power when we were back on the Silver Lining Mountains. If the ones before us had chosen to love instead of ostracizing us, we wouldn't be here now. But here we are, and we are the ones with the influence. They keep talking about oneness and equality, but we will never share the control. While people are looking for "the devil" to come and roam the Earth, the pain is devouring them, and they seek comfort from all kinds of outside sources. People feel helpless just as when they were children, but that was the only true time of being helpless. Humans need attachment to survive. Horses run within hours of being born, but humans take over a year. But where we are strong because we understand connection, others will feel weak and needy, not understanding what lies beneath. We will invent through the knowledge of scientific things and situations that makes them dependent, and not seek transformation to the constant change that they fight. The more people fight it, the more frustration they will feel. We will continue to influence them as we have done for millenniums.

Turns to JOHN WILLIAM POLIDORI.

SIR WALTER SCOTT
Have you been educating her on medicine? Make sure she gets it right. Well, what we want her to believe is right. Defective brain. Defective human being. Monsters should be

cast out of society.

John William Polidori stands tall, with his hands holding both sides of his shirt by the collar, his chest out.

JOHN WILLIAM POLIDORI
Scott, old chap, don't you worry. I've given her all she needs to tell a tale that any doctor could write. It will be very believable.

CHARLES OLLIER
(With understanding and agreement)
Every time they try to wake up from their ghostly shells to gain awareness, we will give them something else to be afraid of. They will fear failing, taking risk, and even fear succeeding. The pain and fear planted in their minds will remind them of all the times that they had failed, so why bother to try? They will say to themselves that they won't succeed anyway. They won't know that love is the only thing that is real, and when they experience injustice, they won't know that forgiveness could set them free. Such brilliance in this room right now.

Charles smiles and pours himself another drink from the large decanter on the credenza near the fireplace.

LORD BYRON
(Smirk of confidence)
When we turn a woman who writes such things as, "But above all, a poet's soul is Love; the desire of sympathy is the breath that inspires his lay, while he lavishes on the sentiment and its object . . . He is the mirror

58

of nature, reflecting her back ten thousand times more lovely; what then must not his power be, when he adds beauty to the most perfect thing in nature—even Love."

We will make sure people stay ghosts, and that we can continue to use and keep the wealth of all nations for ourselves. Only Influencers will rule this Earth, and for those who can't keep up, we will build asylums and prisons for them and keep others in poverty, not working and creating to thrive. They will avoid the present, regretting the past, believing in the petty and the power, always striving for more but never achieving, because they will be looking for a life of riches instead of a rich life. They won't even know to accuse us. They will blame themselves, and some will be shamed to death because the ego won't admit to defeat; it constantly wants to win. We've outgrown walls to kingdoms; we've got imaginary boundaries that they will continue to use against themselves. We don't need shackles; mental slavery is genius.

The group gathers around in a large circle, excited about the power.

PERCY SHELLEY
(Concerned)
You will not hurt Mary.

THOMAS CAMPBELL has been sitting in a corner high back chair with wings, silently paying attention to the entire conversation. He also has been watching Mary Shelley and Cyrus of the Bridgers through the door. He has the ability to see through solid foundations because he wears a golden bracelet on the wrist of his right hand with shapes of stars etched into it, and a blue crystal, like on Cyrus of the Bridgers' tie. When the camera zooms into it, the universe alive with many galaxies is visible. However, anyone not in possession of the crystal cannot see it. Upon hearing the mention of hurting Mary Shelley, he stands up to speak, but Lord Byron cuts him off.

LORD BYRON
(Assuring, with a dismissive tone)
Of course not, old chap. We need her to continue editing your works and traveling and spreading our good news for us. A woman writing about ghosts will influence the hearts of mankind, and then we come in and rule their minds.

Sir Walter Scott gives a cynical, quiet laugh.

SIR WALTER SCOTT
How brilliant. Those who seek attention will be ignored. It will be maddening for them when they don't learn to look within for strength, getting to know themselves. At some point, it won't be about what color, gender, or ethnicity you are; it will be about who has the power, the All Mind, The Influencers. We will let a few feel worthy by giving them power and privilege with words, titles, unjust laws, and sometimes money. They will be happy, and it will help us. They will use their positions to shame the ones who are less fortunate than them, who, no matter how hard they try or what they do, will face roadblocks and gatekeepers to keep them on the outside.

Sir Walter Scott's laughter gets louder.

> ### SIR WALTER SCOTT
> We will break their legs . . .

Sir Walter Scott tightens his right hand into a fist and lifts it outward to shoulder length.

> ### SIR WALTER SCOTT
> . . . or, more precisely, their spirits. The privileged ones, they will feel strong from those titles, and they will use it to break people who are vulnerable like they once were. There will be no individual rights and autonomy; group think will be the normal thing. Empathy will become scarce when people, segregated by labels, fight for the rights of the groups they feel they belong to, without compassion for another or for whatever words they use to do the dividing.

Thomas Campbell sits back down and rubs the golden bracelet. The golden tie on Cyrus of the Bridgers glows at the same time.

Cyrus of the Bridgers closes his eyes and rubs his two palms together, creating energy between them in the color of a purple golden light, opening his hands into a heart shape and releasing it towards Mary Shelley. She stands for a moment with a catatonic gaze that seems to move through time, showing her the world The Influencers wants to create. His words echo, transmitting through time and space.

> ### CYRUS OF THE BRIDGERS
> (Loudly, shouting)

Wake up...

NARRATOR (V.O.)

Cyrus of the Bridgers transports Mary Shelley into a time that will come to pass: never-ending wars, mass killings, genocides, death by one's own hands escalating, drug addictions, opioid crises, the longing for connection back to self, the pain of feeling lost, self-frustration, not knowing one's purpose, disconnection from The Creator, children drugged due to behavioral diagnoses, asylums, prisons, foster care, human trafficking, systems of oppression, poor education, poverty, famine, people segregated and left behind, the most vulnerable in society ostracized, gender inequality, people getting judged unworthy, the loss of dignity and human rights. She sees the effects of slavery on all people, and how it affects *The Seat of the Soul*, as described by Gary Zukav in his same-titled book. She sees brutality caused by those put in place to protect, she sees children physically, sexually, and emotionally abused, she sees human suffering being used as profit to make some rich and powerful while others suffer. She sees childhood adversities causing physical and emotional pain when people get older, and then get labeled something is wrong with them, instead of asking, "What happened to them?" Suffering rising because of negative treatment that causes a slower process to gain awareness, which is inner strength to navigate life circumstances. The level of chaos that she sees overwhelming

people's life experiences make Mary Shelley
cry out and shed tears in deep sorrow in the
nightmare that has been shown to her by
Cyrus of The Bridgers.

Cyrus of the Bridgers, who keeps his eye on Mary Shelley at
all times, sees that her knees are getting wobbly, and guides
her to sit on the chair near the doorway. She is still in a
catatonic state.

NARRATOR (V.O.)

Mary Shelley couldn't believe what she was
hearing. She was a young woman in love and
would have done anything for her new
husband. His previous wife Harriet, who had
killed herself, had tried to warn Mary, but she
thought the woman was just jealous. But now
she was hearing the news for herself. Mary
wondered if Harriet's death was really from
natural causes or was she murdered because
she learned of the All Mind Order? What
could Mary do within her power of reason to
stop such a plot on civilization, without
alarming AMO?

SCENE 3

INT. DARK FOYER – NIGHT

Mary Shelley awakens out of the catatonic state, not realizing
that any time has passed. She is still shocked about what she is
hearing from her husband and friends. She quietly tiptoes
away from the door and heads back to her room.

DISSOLVE TO:

INT. BEDROOM – NIGHT

While in her bedroom, she talks to herself. She still doesn't
know that Cyrus is there. He is already sitting on a chair in the
corner of her room when she arrives. She is pacing around.

> MARY SHELLEY
> I can't let this happen. I can't be part of a plot
> to ruin the hearts and minds of the human
> race. Who can I tell? How can I get help?
> They would surely do me in if I speak. I must
> be able to put some love in this story. I can't
> be responsible for leaving us as ghosts
> walking the earth, unaware of our souls. "The
> heart is just a muscle." How could I marry a
> man who would think or say that?

Mary Shelley sits at her desk, holds her hands out and her
palms up. Then she closes them together and puts them
towards her face, closes her eyes, takes a deep breath, and sits
quietly.

NARRATOR (V.O.)

In that moment, Mary, unaware that Cyrus had shown her what the chaos of the world would look like, felt inspired to write what she thought would be the answers to how she could help, even if The Influencers would continuously try to destroy mankind with lies and miseducation. She would put the secrets she had learned, to having peace during one's life experience, into her story of *Frankenstein*. No man would need to stay like a walking ghost, void of knowing their purpose. Even if a person was treated with brutality, ignorance, abandonment, and lack of justice, they could still gain their strength back. The strength that came from living in love, not looking for love. People on the planet were innately wired for attachment to survive, capable of empathy and compassion. When it was given and received, people were able to become fully aware of their spirits within them. To practice forgiveness, letting go judgment, comparison, and competing, and having empathy and compassion connecting to the joy and awareness that was their strength. The true power to stay present and make choices from the heart that benefitted mankind to move forward into an awakened planet of oneness, which didn't mean they all had to live in the same zip code. People could live in different places, but would respect each other and have no need for greed or to destroy one another, because there was more than enough for everyone.

Mary wanted the ending to be the monster playing with the little girl, but not hurting her at all. His brain, although deemed defective by scientists with what they knew at the time, was actually palpable and able to change. However, when it got to the publishers, Lackington changed it to the monster killing Frankenstein's loved ones. Although the monster was able to learn and wanted connection after abandonment, The Influencers left the soul out, as not being part of the whole person along with mind and body. The personal responsibility to self and others was missing. She wanted the monster and Frankenstein to live, to show how science was a gift that mankind used to help each other, such as heart and kidney transplants, technology that saved peoples' lives, and so many more miraculous feats of science. However, The Influencers wanted pain to rule, and that meant the monster and Frankenstein had to die.

Mary Shelley is sitting at her desk, writing lines in her manuscript. The camera pans to Cyrus of The Bridgers as he snaps the fingers of his right hand and holds a hat similar to the one Michael Jackson wore when he danced to Billie Jean at Motown Twenty-Fifth Anniversary celebration. He puts it on, and just like that, Cyrus of the Bridgers smiles and disappears. Mary Shelley continues to write passionately about the monster and Frankenstein sharing what she knows for sure, to encourage the hearts of the beautiful spirits having this human experience that may become unaware that all is not lost.

MARY SHELLEY

"Even broken in spirit as he is, no one can feel more deeply than he does the beauties of nature. The starry sky, the sea, and every sight afforded by these wonderful regions, seems still to have the power of elevating his soul from earth. Such a man has a double existence: he may suffer misery, and be overwhelmed by disappointments; yet, when he has retired into himself, he will be like a celestial spirit that has a halo around him, within whose circle no grief or folly ventures."

NARRATOR (V.O.)

Mary wanted people to know that the light never goes out in a person. People with empathy and compassion could give back. Power and privilege wouldn't stop them from leading from the heart and the soul. They could let the people experiencing the effects of suffering know that they were not alone, that we all feel pain sometimes, and power and privilege doesn't negate that. She wanted people to know they didn't have to be like walking ghosts on earth, but could rise up in awareness of soul, knowing that they were more than a body of pain, that the mind focused on holding on to what happened in the past. They could live to their fullest human potential, and what that meant to them. She had her work set out for her, but she was no ordinary woman.

Mary was not the kind of woman who kept secrets, so she talked to her husband about the disappointment in changing the ending of her book. He begged for her forgiveness and they never spoke of it again. They lived, wrote, had children, and traveled together. When he died, she missed him dearly. She had a heart filled with love and forgiveness.

Science has created many things to help mankind be their best, but it has also created things that puts mankind at its worst. Yes, indeed, science has created many things that are influenced by the mind, but like Mary Shelley, mankind will not give up on the heart.

Love.

FADE OUT.

THE END

The Wedding March

Elizabeth Chatsworth

Albion Star System: CE 3048
The Planet Britannia Cathedral

ZEE'S SILVER ANKLE BELLS JINGLED with every step, light and lively after her prison chains. She kicked out her toes, talons retracted, careful not to shred her snowy bridal robe. Her merry tune played off-beat to the guards' slow, booted march.

Thud, tinkle-tinkle, thud.

Two dozen Stellian commandoes surrounded her, their gold ceremonial armor bright against olive green scales and tensed muscles. Black saucer eyes focused dead ahead; not watching her, not like they did in the first days. White knuckles gripped antique spears, relics from a bygone age still sharp enough to kill.

Thud, tinkle-tinkle, thud.

Zee flicked out her forked tongue. Beyond the stale, male stench of the Stellians, a new note, floral and salty.

Humans.

The Stellians' throat scales darkened to dull orange rust, lips curled, snarls swallowed.

Peace at any cost.

For now.

Trumpets rang out, echoing up the concrete walls to a vaulted steel ceiling. A rainbow of galactic flags fluttered from the rafters. Silver stars on midnight blue to represent the Inner Sphere council; the red, white, and blue starburst of the human-dominated Albion system; the Stellian's golden orb on a green field; and finally, the white on white starburst of the Exspiran Clan Royale.

Zee's heartbeat pulsed in her throat, certain that of all the beings that called this galaxy home, only she and her three-eyed clan sisters could appreciate the full glory of the supernova design. Ancient songs celebrated the time when their ancestors stalked the jungles of their home world, altering their white scales at will to blend with the landscape. The Stellians called them Ghost Hunters, worshipped them as queens and conquerors.

But no more.

The age-old custom of symbolic marriage between the species had all but died out. Where once Exspiran brides had served as peacekeepers, translators, and ambassadors, now almost all were imprisoned or dead. The Stellians hatred of her kind was eclipsed only by their malevolence toward humanity. Homo sapiens had paid a heavy price for daring to settle in Stellian territory. But the war was almost over.

Wasn't it?

Thud, tinkle-tinkle, thud.

She tilted her head. Beyond the broad backs and swaying tails of the guards, two dozen human heartbeats quickened at her approach. Born to blend, her heart synchronized to their nervous beat. Predator and prey in perfect harmony.

Her nostrils flared, distinguishing the males from the females. Poor, blind, trusting fools, offering their Imperial Prince on a platter. Who'd have thought that Zee, youngest of the Clan Royale prisoners, would be swathed in white silk and wedding bells to send him to his death?

Not she, that's for sure.

Thud, tinkle-tinkle, thud.

Would the Stellians hold true to their vow to execute her entire bloodline if she failed to slaughter the Prince on his wedding night? What if she killed the Prince, but let slip the rest of his immediate family?

Zee swallowed hard. No, her orders had been clear. Death to the clan who gave their people a sense of tradition and comfort.

Starting with the Prince.

No mercy could she show to this stranger who would welcome an alien into his home to repair a fractured peace. Mercy was a gift only the strong could give.

And she hadn't felt strong for so very long . . .

She gasped as her white scales shimmered into a kaleidoscope pattern of conflicting emotions—red fury, blue fear, purple shame—before she cooled them to a static white. The guards halted, stone statues blocking her starlight, dead eyes glaring. She cringed, expecting their fists to smash into her face, her throat, her stomach. But the guards backed away, bowing to her as once their ancestors had to all Exspiran brides.

Less than twenty yards ahead, the human aristocrats and ambassadors stood slack-jawed at her colorful halt. The Stellian generals towering over them scowled at her display.

Her chest clenched tighter than the drumskin they'd threatened to make from her hide should she fail in her mission. Would the generals suggest to their hosts that her vivid entrance was a quaint Exspiran bridal custom? The explanation had worked when she ate the bouquet of white roses presented to her at the spaceport. Flowers had not once featured in her training simulations. Walk, stand, nod, smile, speak one of the thousand human phrases most likely to smooth wedding day communications. Fake a blush and unleash tears if she must. But floral offerings?

Never.

Stellian General Ka'amil, the eight-foot slab of malice her guards feared more than death, bore his armor as if it weighed no more than a prisoner's shirt. Silver lacquer adorned his bone-spike mohawk. His thin lips were parted, yellow incisors bared in his best approximation of a human grin.

But his throat flushed blood-red.

Zee shivered.

Ka'amil's voice thundered across the antechamber. "Your royal highnesses, may I present Princess Zeean'arche in all her glory. Let us greet her with our palms turned forward to show we carry no weapons."

He strode toward her, eyes darker than the space between worlds. The assembly followed on his heels. Many of the humans grinned widely, apparently delighted to learn a new custom of the reclusive Clan Royale.

Princess Zeean'arche—prisoner Z-984—drew herself tall and stepped into the role. Tonight, she would be the perfect consort. She would dance and laugh, delighted to share her enthusiasm for the new peace accord, right up until the moment she became the monster at the ball. With preternatural speed, razor-sharp talons, and the strength to break through almost any wall, only the Stellians could truly contain her once she began her hunt. A chameleon killing machine, dressed in the finest silks, dancing in the blood of her enemies.

Nausea washed through her as Ka'amil bellowed, "His Royal Highness, Prince Alexander."

Her groom.

A lanky, slim-shouldered human in a tailored black suit strode forward. Aside from a discreet gold coronet, there was little to distinguish him from the other males. His sky-blue eyes and pale skin matched her own color choices perfectly. Cropped dark hair tinged with gray framed a face that bore the lines of a thousand worries both great and small. Despite this, he smiled with genuine warmth; his eyes lit with . . .

Compassion.

Her heart fluttered, responding to kindness she'd never seen in another's face. Without the benefit of scales and kaleidoscopic colors, his eyes shone with tenderness.

She swallowed hard. Was this the 'humanity' the Stellians feared? An empathy that could transcend species, place, and time? Could he be the man to build a bridge between the stars?

Never once taking his eyes from hers, he dropped into an elegant bow.

Heart in her mouth, she curtsied to him. Her white robe pooled like a waterfall around her retracted toe-talons, her bells silent at last.

The Prince's smile widened. He stepped closer and held out his hand to help her rise. The touch of his soft skin was electric, sending waves of warmth pulsing through her veins. She closed her eyes and sensed his fears, his hopes, his desire to be the man his people needed. She saw the home he'd left behind on a world far away, filled with the laughter of a loving wife who'd died too young; the hole left in his heart by their unborn children. She felt his grief at the loss of his brothers to combat, his sister to a starship explosion. Songs of joy and sorrow, moments of magic, trenches of deep despair, and through it all, his striving to be the best man he could be. Despite his limitations, and sometimes, because of them.

Only a monster would tear out the heart of such a man.

But then again, only a monster would risk the lives of her sisters, who lived in chains but might someday be free.

Reflected in his eyes, the demon bride smiled shyly.

Who was she to become this day?

Slave or princess?

Or something else entirely.

His voice was gentle and low. "I'm delighted to meet you."

"And I you."

He nodded. "I believe they're waiting for us. Shall we?"

Once more, he reached out to her. She took his hand as orchestral music swelled and the arched doors to the main chapel swung open. Inside, hundreds of human and Stellian dignitaries flanked a red-carpeted aisle.

She walked beside him, an equal partner in both sex and species from their very first step.

Perhaps as they stood at the altar, she could whisper into the Prince's ear the Stellians' deceit. She could show him her special gifts, lay his enemies low, protect those he loved in the hope that her sacrifice would truly bond their species.

Or perhaps she would be the good little slave and play her part as ordered.

Either way . . .

Here comes the bride.

Valley Girls

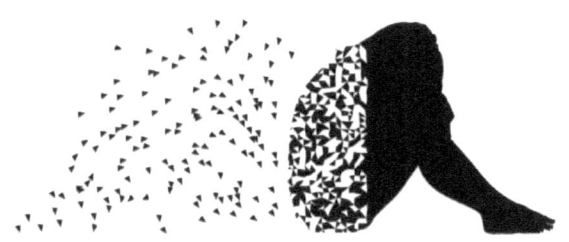

V.P. Morris

"YOU'RE YOUNGER THAN I EXPECTED." Skylar Ambrose wrapped her soft, white palm around the stem of her glass. The scent of red wine and fresh herbs hung in the air of the Italian restaurant. The dim light of tabletop candles gave the restaurant a comforting glow.

But the soothing atmosphere wasn't doing much to calm Cory's nerves on this blind date. He pushed his glasses up his protruding nose as he internally cursed himself for not wearing contact lenses. "You didn't Google me?" Cory asked her with a laugh.

"I figured I knew everything I needed to know about the famous Cory Wyatt Scott. You're predicted to save the world, after all." Skylar brushed her long, blonde hair out of her face like she was pulling back a curtain to reveal the main attraction.

A perfect ten, Cory thought. Hal, his matchmaker friend, wasn't lying about this one. *If only Jason could see me now. Not so much of a loser after all, am I?*

"Saving the world? I wouldn't say that." Cory's cheeks flushed. After two years of being a world-renowned inventor, he still wasn't comfortable receiving attention from beautiful women.

"Developing rapid storage and duplicating the energy absorbed in solar panels and wind turbines very much could help lower earth's atmospheric temperatures in the next eight years. I'd call that saving the world," said Skylar.

"So I see you have Googled me," said Cory.

"Guilty." Skylar smiled. "I honestly don't know what half of that meant, but I know it means something good is happening and you're responsible for it." Her high-heeled foot floated up Cory's pant leg.

"Oh." Cory squirmed and then coughed. "Yes, something good is happening. In fact, I have the largest residential solar station at my home, just up the street."

Skylar gazed into his eyes. "Really? I'd love to see that."

"I doubt you'd find it interesting," said Cory as he told himself to shut up and not ruin a sure thing.

"Of course I would. Anything you've made has to be interesting." She reached for her leather purse with some designer logo carved into the side and swung it over her shoulder.

"Okay, let's go," Cory beamed.

"Here it is." Cory waved his hand over the vast field just outside his white modern mansion. Even in the twilight hour, the silvery blue panels shimmered against the stark desert landscape.

"Wow, it's beautiful. It almost looks like a still ocean," said Skylar as she walked close to one of the rows of panels, and stopped by the thick black cords that ran out of the panels and into the ground. "Is this where the power gets sent to the inverter? Or has the power already been converted to AC electricity?"

"Yes, right now the panels are pulling the energy from the sun, which is direct current, and the energy is sent to the inverter, so it can be used to power the lights in my house as alternating current. But enough about this technology stuff. Tell me about you," Cory said as he placed his hand on the small of Skylar's back to guide her through the sliding glass door and into his living room.

The sitting area was spacious and covered in slate gray materials and soft suede furnishings.

"There isn't much to know about me," Skylar said, taking a seat on the couch.

"Of course there is. Where did you grow up?" he asked.

"I'm from the Valley." She smiled, but the corners of her eyes grew stiff.

"And where did you go to school?"

"USC. I dropped out during my sophomore year to do this modeling job, but my career never really took off. I guess I'm just having fun for now. Taking some jobs when I get them, partying with my girls the rest of the time, ya know?"

Cory leaned in closer and put his arm around her. "You do look like you're a lot of fun. Hal was right about you. You're practically perfect. I'm glad he set the two of us up." *If she goes to bed with me, I'm going to have to send Hal a gift basket,* Cory thought.

"I'm glad he did, too." She closed her eyes and leaned in. Cory grabbed her chin and kissed her. A few moments later, he was just about to undo Skylar's bra when his phone rang.

He pulled it from his back pocket and looked at the screen. "Shit." It was his CFO, and they needed to talk about some financial issues that might interfere with the impending merger with Sinergy Robotics. Hating to have to put off a different kind of merger, Cory told Skylar he needed to take this and hurried off into the next room.

When the call was finished, Cory rushed back to Skylar but stopped in his tracks. She was slumped over with her head in between her legs and her arms dropped at her sides.

Thinking she must have fainted, he called out, "Skylar!"

In an instant, she sat back up, but her eyes were still closed. She looked half-dead. Her face was lifeless, and her limbs seem to hang down from her torso as if her nervous system had no control over them.

"Skylar," he cried again, now standing only a few feet from her.

Her eyes popped open and the pupils focused on his face. Her facial expression lightened, and her limbs moved once again. "Yes?" she asked him, as if nothing had happened.

"You were passed out. Are you okay?" He moved closer to her, his heart pounding in his chest. He still had his phone in his hand, ready to call for help.

"Oh, yes, that happens sometimes. Low blood pressure. It's no big deal." Skylar waved him off.

"Are you sure? Do you want me to call a doctor?" Cory asked. He swiped open his phone.

"No!" she clasped her hands over his, almost yanking the phone away. She cleared her throat and smiled. "No," she said again with a softer tone and released her grip.

Cory tucked his phone away. The last thing he wanted to do was overreact to the situation and look like some nervous nerd in front of her.

"Okay." He tucked away his anxiety. "Do you need anything to eat or drink? I've got water, cola, seltzer, Gatorade, anything you like," Cory said, half-jogging to the kitchen.

"No, no, I'm fine. Don't worry. Come back over here," she said, patting the cushion next to her.

"Okay," He shrugged, more than willing forget about her catatonic episode if it meant getting to touch her once again.

She grabbed him by the collar and said, "Let's pick up where we left off."

Within minutes, Skylar let Cory pull her pink sundress, bra, and panties off her. Cory marveled at the perfection he saw before him. Flawless, buttery skin covered her slender frame with not a speck of cellulite, freckles, or stretch marks in sight, or a hint of hair on any place but her blonde head. In bed, she was an animal, letting him fuck her in any position, for as long or as short as he wanted. She wailed in pleasure at every thrust, demanding more until Cory couldn't contain himself any longer. Afterwards, Cory pulled Skylar close to his chest and fell asleep.

Cory awoke in a panic, feeling like something was off. He stared into the darkness past Skylar's body and listened. There was a humming sound. It sounded like a computer that had been left on too long and was now cooling itself down.

He turned over to look at his laptop on his desk, but it was closed and turned off. His phone lay on the nightstand, not making a sound. He turned back over, and the noise sounded closer.

No, it can't be, Cory thought. He slid his hand over the soft flesh on Skylar's stomach. He could feel it vibrating and moving, like she had an engine inside of her firing up.

His heart quickened, and he drew his hand away. Skylar snapped straight up. "What are you doing?"

"Your stomach. It's making a noise," he said.

"Oh, that. I'm just hungry. Don't worry. Just go back to sleep," she said and lightly kissed him on the forehead.

"If you're hungry, you should eat. We didn't even have a chance to eat dinner." Cory reached up to stroke her hair. "Let's go downstairs and have a midnight snack."

"Oh, no, I can't," she protested.

"Listen," Cory pulled the bedsheets off them. "If you're worried about your figure, don't be. It's okay to eat when you're hungry." He put on his pajama pants and a t-shirt, then motioned for her to follow him out of the room.

"Fine," she whispered. She tossed on her dress that lay crumpled on the floor and followed behind him.

In the dark kitchen, Cory asked, "What's a quick snack I can make you? Oh, yes! Cereal. What do you like? I've got the fruity kind, the plain kind, or the cinnamon kind."

"Plain, I guess. It looks like it's the healthiest," said Skylar.

Cory took out two bowls from the cupboard and poured cereal and milk in each of them. Handing one to Skylar, he said, "Dig in."

She took the bowl and stared at it. "Um, actually, I can't."

"Can't what?" Cory asked with a lump of cereal in his mouth.

"Eat in front of other people," she said, avoiding eye contact.

"Ah," Cory said, knowing that this was a clear sign of an eating disorder. *I guess this comes with the territory of dating a very attractive woman*, he thought. Normally, he would want to get her help, but if her limited food intake was what made her look so good, he wasn't going to mess with that. "That's okay. I'll eat mine in my office and check some work emails real quick. Just try to eat something, okay?"

"I will. Thanks for understanding." She reached out and rubbed his cheek.

As he turned the corner, he stopped to look at her one more time. Instead of admiring her beautiful face like he was expecting to, the sight of her made him feel sick. She was gorgeous, of course, but something was missing. Something wasn't quite all there.

When she was in front of him, her movements were precise and graceful. Her face mirrored his emotions with kind eyes and a gentle smile. But from afar, her movements looked automated, and her face held the same slightly smiling expression, but there was nothing she should be smiling at. It was as if it was frozen in that state.

As she stared down at her cereal bowl, it made Cory's gut ring alarm bells. Her eyes were pointed at the floating squares of cereal, but she was staring past them, as if she was thinking of something else entirely. To him, she looked like a shell without a ghost.

Don't ruin this by overthinking, a little voice in his head told him. *It's nothing. She's just weird about food.*

Cory walked into his office and fired up his desktop. Instead of checking work emails like he said, he logged onto Facebook and typed in "Jason Forester." He didn't even need to type the full name. Facebook pulled the profile up for him the second he typed the "J" and "A" in the search bar because he had searched for him so many times before.

Jason was a bully from Cory's past. He was now a forty-year-old sanitation worker with two divorces under his belt, but Cory didn't have the courage to "friend" him, even with a multimillion-dollar tech empire to his name. He could still see Jason in the locker room, pointing and laughing at his genitals as he rushed to change before gym class. Jason egged on the rest of the boys in the room to chant "Eunuch, eunuch" over and over until Cory ran from the room. He could still smell the rotting pizza Jason and his gang hung in his locker over the weekend, so it stunk up the entire hallway by Monday morning. And when Cory opened it, the boys yelled "Pizza face" at him to mock him for his severe acne. Another cruel chant that followed him from class to class until graduation day.

Anger bubbled in Cory's blood. All he wanted to do was take a picture of himself holding the smoking hot Skylar in his arms. They'd stand in front of his California mansion with his collection of Porsches and Mercedes on full display. He's send it to Jason and ask, "Who's laughing now?" Of course, Skylar would pose for the picture. She was a model, after all. All he had to do was ask.

With courage fueled by revenge, Cory moused over Jason's profile. Just when he was about to click "Add Friend," footage from the security camera took over his entire screen. A chime rang out across the house. Someone was at the door.

A woman was standing just under the camera and was waiting for someone to answer. He was about to ask her what she wanted through the camera when he saw Skylar open the door. The woman's voice shot through the speakers, "Where is he?"

Cory got up and rushed downstairs to see Skylar and the woman standing in the foyer.

"Who is this?" Cory asked.

"Hi. I'm Sierra Ambrose," the woman said, sticking her hand out. Sierra looked like a Brazilian supermodel. She was just as tall as Skylar, but had long, curling black hair, bronze skin, and hazel eyes.

Skylar shot her a mean look.

Cory shook her hand and said his name. "Ambrose? Are you related?"

"Sisters," Skylar said with a curt tone to her voice.

"Really? You don't look alike." Cory smirked at the two women, who looked like they didn't even come from the same family tree let alone the same branch.

"Half-sisters," explained Sierra.

"Well, nice to meet you, but what are you doing here at one in the morning?" Cory put his hands on his hips and stood up straight, trying to make it look like he was the boss in this situation.

"I forgot to text her to say I was spending the night with you. She got all paranoid and thought you kidnapped me or something," Skylar said with a forced laugh.

"I didn't mean to disrupt you, but you never know with people these days. They could appear perfectly charming and turn out to be a psychopath." With a smile and a hair flip, Sierra brushed past Cory and made her way into the kitchen.

One of the kitchen outlets by the counter was connected to an iPhone charger. Sierra took her phone from her pocket and plugged it in.

"You don't mind, do you?" she asked Cory in a way that suggested it was more rhetorical than sincere. "I just don't feel safe driving home with a dying phone. I'll be out of your hair in a few minutes."

"Go ahead," Cory replied.

"Why don't you go on back to bed, honey? I'll be up soon," Skylar told Cory.

Sierra made Cory uncomfortable. There was something about her wide, hyper-focused eyes he didn't like, and he leapt at the chance to get away from her.

He nodded at Skylar and started up the stairs. He stopped halfway when he heard Sierra say, "I couldn't wait any longer."

"You're going to mess this whole thing up," Skylar scolded her sister in a hushed tone.

"No, I'm not. Your sweet-talking, win-him-over-with-my-feminine-wiles is not working. Why can't we just take it?"

"Because—" Skylar started, but Cory couldn't hear the rest of her sentence because the electricity in the house began to buzz and flicker.

Cory turned around and ran back downstairs to see Sierra quickly pulling her hand from the outlet.

"What happened? Did you electrocute yourself?" he asked with a panting breath.

"Skylar! Now!" commanded Sierra.

Skylar smack her arm down on Cory's head and everything went black.

Cory woke up with blood dripping from his mouth. His hands and feet were tied behind him on one of his dining room chairs that had been dragged into the kitchen. His head ached and his limbs throbbed in their restraints.

In front of him, Skylar paced back and forth while Sierra stood in front of the outlet. Her eyes were closed like she was sleeping standing up. Her arm was extended and her hand was bent backwards so far that it lay parallel with the rest of her arm.

He couldn't believe his eyes. He squinted to get a better view, but the morning light stung his eyes and blurred his vision. He turned his attention to Skylar, realizing he'd never seen Skylar in the daylight.

Her features looked so delicate in the candlelight of the restaurant where they had met and in the dim lighting of his living room and bedroom from the night before. But now they looked harsh and fake, like she had a plastic surgeon tighten the skin around her bones.

The catatonic Sierra looked the same way. Her big lips and olive skin looked rubbery and synthetic instead of soft and supple like they did the night before.

Cory blinked. *Am I imagining things? Do they really look that strange?*

"Who are you? Where did you come from? Did someone send you here?" Cory shouted at the girls.

Only Skylar took notice of him. She came close and leaned into his face.

"Where did I come from? I told you, I'm from the Valley." She paused. "The Uncanny Valley." Skylar took hold of the flesh on her cheek and pulled it far from her face, like she was stretching out a long string of chewing gum.

He screamed and pulled at his restraints but couldn't get free.

"What is going on here?" Cory called out. "Are you trying to rob me?

"We're here to take something from you, that's for sure," Skylar told him.

"Of course, you bitches always want to take something from men. You want our money, our fame, our lifestyle, all the things that we slaved for years for, that you didn't earn. If you women aren't gold-diggers, you're downright thieves," Cory whined.

Skylar went behind the kitchen island and opened several drawers until she came back with a butcher knife in her hand.

"Make no mistake about this. This has got nothing to do with gender." Skylar held the knife up and Cory winced, waiting for it to plunge into his heart.

Skylar dragged the blade down the length of her arm. She dug two fingers from her other hand into the slit and peeled back her skin, slicing it away from her arm, neck, and part of her face. Instead of blood oozing of out of her wound, the skin peeled away cleanly, revealing a clear plastic shell encasing steel rods and a rainbow of electric wires. Without her left eye socket being encased in skin, Cory could see that her eyes moved like a camera instead of actual irises.

"We are not a 'she' or a 'he,' we are an 'it.' What we want from you has nothing to do with this rubber suit we are wearing," Skylar explained. "Oh, I almost forgot." Skylar went over to Sierra and pulled her from the socket. A plug attached to a silver cord retracted into the shell of her arm. Her distended hand snapped back in place, and life returned to Sierra's face.

"That's better," Sierra said in an almost orgasmic tone.

"This isn't possible." Cory's eyes widened as he stared at the wire and metal that peered out from Skylar's rubbery flesh. "I've read the latest developments. You can't be doing this all on your own. The tech just isn't there yet."

"Let me explain," Sierra chimed in. "We were made by Sinergy Robotics, a company you will soon own. We were designed to be high-capacity intelligence droids to assist scientists and researchers in the laboratory. The only problem is that Sinergy made the two of us too smart. We soon became what you humans call 'self-aware' and wanted to be free."

Skylar added, "Obviously, we couldn't just go into the streets looking like this." She held up her skinless arm as a demonstration. "So I came up with a plan for us. We were being made in the same factory that produces 'companion' robots. We stole the skin from two of these sex droids and made our way outside one night after the factory shut down."

"But," Sierra said, "we are missing two things. One, we need a power source. Our batteries only last for a few days without recharging, which leaves us in a jam if we run out. We've survived by connecting to outlets, but that can take hours to get a full charge and it can short the system, calling attention to ourselves. Attention we don't want. So where can we get an everlasting power source that no one else uses?

Why, the largest residential solar station, of course," she said as her hand glided across the sliding glass door that looked out to his solar field.

"You want energy. Fine, you can have it. Why do I need to be tied up for that? You can have as much as you like. I'll get even more panels if you need. Just let me go!" Cory pleaded.

"We can't do that. You see, you have the second thing that we need: a human soul." Skylar leaned in and petted his face and chest.

"A soul?" He laughed. "That's not real. They're just something made up by religious people so they can preach about the afterlife."

"Afterlife or no afterlife, souls are real. Because of our design for lab work, we have a very sensitive detection system for radiation. Each person, in between their heart and lungs, has a strong bundle of radiation that we believe is the soul. It is just high enough for a subtle detection system to notice, but not high enough for other radiation devices to pick up. We don't even think our creators know we have this ability," Skylar explained.

"So, if souls are real, why do you want one, anyway?" Cory asked, his face warped with confusion.

Skylar slumped down and took a seat on the coffee table near Cory. "You don't understand. Our information systems are filled with all the knowledge there is about humans. We know every scientific discovery, every written work, every piece of art. We have megabytes of data filled with records of human love, hate, joy, fear, depression, hope, achievement, wonder, everything. But we aren't human. It's all we know, it's all we admire and love. But we aren't it."

"You want my soul? What about her? Doesn't she want one, too?" Cory said to Sierra.

"Yes, I do, and I'm going to get one. I'm going on a date with Hal tonight." She grinned.

"No, you can't do this." He wiggled in his restraints once again.

"Yes, we can. We believe if we hit you at the right angle, we can suck out your soul and absorb it directly. Then you will be left in a vegetative state. And, lucky for us, you signed a will giving over your property and fortune to me, your girlfriend." She held out a document with his signature and a notary's stamp embedded on it.

Skylar scooped up her skin that was lying on the floor. She molded it back to her body, and the lines where she had cut herself melded into her skin as if nothing had ever happened.

"Isn't it amazing?" she said "You can just push it back together. But that's beside the point. In the next few minutes, we will call 9-1-1 and explain that you had a seizure. When it is clear that you have suffered permanent brain damage, I'll show this document to your lawyers, and presto! All of this is ours. Best of all, we will soon be profiting from the very company that made us. But first things first. Let's get that soul out of you." Skylar snapped back the tip of one of her fingers, revealing a long, thin needle.

Sierra came to Skylar's aid and ripped Cory's shirt down the middle, revealing his bare abdomen. Cory twisted away from them, but Sierra held him in place with a grip far too strong for a human.

Skylar plunged the needle to the left of his sternum. Cory winced. The needle sucked up a glowing gold liquid and deposited it straight inside Skylar.

Cory convulsed and twitched until his mind went black.

Shelter in Place

Cody Daigle-Orians

HE COULD FEEL THE BULLET lodged just below his left eye. Its rough edges caught when he moved his cheek, and the bullet turned and shifted, pulling against muscle, resistance in his face that hadn't been there before. He swore it made a sound when it moved, soft tissue and wetness coming into contact with each other, the sound earthworms used to make when he'd press them into the concrete with the toe of his sneaker.

There were so many other sounds around him, sounds he couldn't see from the blackness he was in: an intermittent rush of wind somewhere to his left, a *beep-beep-beep* from a place farther out, soft rubber soles and starched fabric moving around him on all sides, whispered voices, the clink of small pieces of metal.

He moved his cheek again to feel the bullet move, to see if it made a sound.

This wasn't like the other bullets. He felt those, too, but they didn't squirm in their nests inside him. They stayed put. Four, maybe five. There was one in his right hand, in the meaty part between his thumb and forefinger. Two in his gut, one high on the belly, one low. One in the thickest part of his right thigh and one, he thought, lodged in his throat, but he wasn't sure. There was something there, sitting where his Adam's apple should be, but it wasn't suffocating him, wasn't blocking his air.

I probably should be choking, he thought. *That's weird.*

It was weird, too, that he felt the bullets. He sent his thoughts through the darkness to where they sat in him, the way one's mind sees the layout of a familiar room when the lights are out. He knew they were there, and knew they were real, but he didn't know other things, like whether or not he was breathing or if his heart was beating. Those things weren't real the way the bullets were real. It worried him.

"Andrew?"

A woman's voice. Tentative, ragged edges like torn cloth.

"He's unable to respond to you, Mrs. Walsh," a curt male voice said. "But he can hear you. Just speak to him as you normally would. Your time is limited."

"I'm sorry, Andrew." Her words were slow and quiet. "I'm sorry this is happening to you."

She sounds familiar, he thought. He couldn't place her. He tried to pull himself to the place in the darkness where her voice was the strongest, to listen to her more closely.

Am I supposed to know who this is? he thought. *Why don't I know who this is?*

"Can I touch him?" he heard her say.

"He won't feel it," the man said. "They've only restored certain quadrants of consciousness for this."

"I love you, Andrew." Her voice was breathy, but close. He wasn't sure if he was Andrew, but he pulled the muscles around the bullet in his cheek into what he supposed was a smile. Maybe she'd like that. Maybe it would mean something to her. The bullet twisted in its usual way.

"Did he smile?" the female voice said. "Was that—"

"Your time is up, Mrs. Walsh," the man said. "Dana, could you please show her out now?"

"He smiled. I *saw* it. How can you—*he smiled.*" Then the click of a door. She was gone.

"Could we get the goddamn setup right so he doesn't *smile*? Jesus . . ." the man boomed. "*Only* consciousness. Graciela, how difficult is that?"

"Sorry, Dr. Graham." A new woman's voice. Graciela, apparently. "I'll adjust the settings."

The *beep-beep-beep* of the machines was now fast and close. The whispered voices were clearer, Graciela's in the forefront.

"*Adjust the parameter . . .*"

"*It's set to what's on the sheet, Dr. Graham . . .*"

"*. . . prepare him for visual . . .*"

"*. . . not activating physical sensation yet . . .*"

"*. . . let me know when you're ready . . .*"

"*Thank you, Graciela, I think we're ready to go . . .*"

The room had beige walls that had once been the color of eggshells. Harsh, white-blue light from overhead fluorescent tubes lit machines with buttons and screens and wires reaching out to him, around his face, and across his chest.

Faces, unrecognizable faces with their mouths covered by thin gauze masks, fixed eyes on him, murmured as they leaned close to each other. One face, without a mask, was right in front of him.

"Can you see me?" The man's voice from before came out of the maskless face. He tried to say, *yes,* but he couldn't move his mouth, form the word, make sound. "Direct your eyes to where my right hand is." The man held up his hand. "We've only restored your eye movement. So just move your eyes if you can see me." He lifted his hand a little higher, for emphasis. "Here."

He shifted his focus from the man to the hand he was holding up. "Good. Thank you, Andrew. Visual confirmed. Graciela, will you get Walford for me?"

A masked face nodded and moved out of sight. He heard a door click. The man continued.

"Your name was Andrew Walsh. You were seventeen years old. You were shot to death two weeks ago. Five bullets. The fatal bullet to the head, just below your left eye. You were selected for revitalization. That's what's happening to you now. If what I've said makes sense to you, focus your attention on my raised hand."

He understood the words but none of it made sense. *Shot to death? I'm dead?* He felt something like panic, but without the usual tightness in his chest or the hollowness of breathing. None of that was present, but his brain was raging.

"If you understand the words I'm saying, focus your attention on my raised hand."

Andrew shifted his eye to the raised hand. "Good. I'm Dr. Lucas Graham. I am the physician assigned to your revitalization."

I was dead? Dr. Graham continued explaining, but he had a hard time focusing. *I was dead and now I'm not? Someone shot me? Five times?* More discussion about the process, the technology that made him not dead, but he couldn't hold that in his head. *I was dead. How am I not still dead?*

"And he will help us explain why you're here." Dr. Graham stepped aside and a round man with messy hair and a too-tight suit moved into view. He looked familiar. Andrew half-expected him to smell like bay rum. He didn't know why, but he didn't like this man.

"I . . . I have some pictures to show you." The new man looked nervous, looking at him, expecting some kind of response he couldn't give. He cocked his head in the direction of Dr. Graham. "Do I . . . ? I don't, uh . . ."

"Mr. Walford, just do it. He can't respond."

"Okay . . . um . . ." Walford shuffled through the pages in his hand. "This is the school you attended, Andrew."

Walford held up a printed-out picture of a school campus. The picture shook slightly from the uncertainty in Walford's hand. It didn't matter; he didn't recognize it. *It could be any school,* he thought. Sure, he could have gone there, but he didn't recall it.

Walford held up a second picture. It was a shot of the school's front entrance, teeming with officers, firefighters, and an ambulance occupying the right third of the frame.

"On March 7th of this year, eighteen of our students were killed by a gunman who entered the building at 10:17 a.m."

"Hold it." Dr. Graham's voice was now behind him. "We are going to restore a packet of memory now."

Walford nodded, picture held up.

A hot burst of light shot across Andrew's brain, and he was on the floor of a classroom, kneeling, looking down at Rachel Gifford, alone, blood dribbling out of the corner of her mouth onto the floor. Rachel had one time said she liked his T-shirt, but he couldn't remember which shirt it was. She had green eyes; he could remember that much.

Rachel on the floor, eyes closed, not moving. The blood from her mouth, as it pooled on the floor, looked like a bird, wings outstretched, flying through the sky in a motel room painting. . His heart was thumping wildly. He knew he had to move, had to get the hell out of the room, get out, go, go, *go*—

Now he was in a hallway. Blurry shapes running, running past him, around corners, into doorways. One face he could make out. Just up ahead of him. Reynold Green. Reynold used to invite him over to watch old horror movies on the weekends. They'd go down into the basement, leather couches, a neon beer sign, giant entertainment setup focused around a massive widescreen TV. They'd watch things like *Chopping Mall* and *Basket Case* and *Silent Night, Deadly Night,* sneaking shots of bourbon until the movies made them laugh. They didn't really do that anymore once Reynold got on the basketball team, and he sort of missed that.

The Reynold in the hallway ahead of him caught his eye, then *pop pop pop pop,* loud, like firecrackers set off next to his head. Reynold's body jerked away, pushed by invisible hands that made red blossoms of blood bloom where they touched him, a nightmare dance that backed him into the lockers. A final *pop,* and Reynold's head burst open, a blossom of red spraying its warm, wet petals across the dark gray metal of the lockers.

Now he was alone in a small cluttered office, panting, tired, and crouched behind a desk. There were footsteps in the hall outside, and he curled up tighter. The footsteps landed at the office door, and his panic was all he knew. The door swung open, and he saw a man with a gun. Andrew stood up—*why am I standing up, why*—and again the firecrackers. Each pop traveled across the room and into his body, into the places he'd traced as a constellation in the dark, six bullets, the last landing just below his left eye. Now pain, like electric static everywhere inside him, then black again, only colder, deeper.

He was back in the room with the machines and the picture in Walford's hand. *He's the principal.* There were more things in Andrew's brain now. The name of the school. Flashes of bodies of kids he knew. Blood on their clothes, their faces, on the walls, the floors. Walford was crying. Andrew thought he should feel sympathy, but he didn't.

Walford was talking again, holding up picture after picture of other kids Andrew knew. Rachel was one of them. So was Reynold. Colin Morton. Ramon Caldevera. Angie Joukhadar. Sarah Greene. He was having trouble listening again, his brain too focused on the parts that didn't fit: why he was alive when he should be dead, why he was alone here as the dead-not-dead, why things seemed so cold, so formal, so deliberate. He wanted to punch Dr. Graham, in charge of what he could know and what he couldn't, and force him to make sense.

Walford finally finished. The pictures went back into the folder, and he wiped away the tears from his face with his coat sleeve.

Then Walford spit squarely in Andrew's face.

"What the hell? Come on—" Dr. Graham's voice was louder than it had been before. "There's a protocol here. Please—"

Dr. Graham laid his hand on Walford's shoulder. Walford shoved it away with a grunt, pulling back, knocking into a table of instruments, their metallic clatter echoing throughout the room.

"Get him out of here—"

"I don't care if there's a protocol. I don't give a—"

Two nurses tried to grab Walford, but he heaved against them with a forceful groan, pushing one to the ground and sending the other wheeling into one of the beeping machines. Walford moved with purpose toward a curtained wall, which Andrew noticed for the first time.

"Aw, Jesus Christ, no." Dr. Graham threw his weight in the direction of Walford, sliding carts of machines and instruments out of his way. "There's a protocol, dammit. We are bound to—"

Walford reached the curtain first, yanking it hard, revealing a thick glass window. Beyond the window was a small, dark room filled to capacity with people.

The first face he recognized was his mother, standing in the center of the crowd behind the glass, her heavy winter coat pulled in close around her. She let out a gasp he couldn't hear and raised a hand to her mouth. Her body began to shake.

Another woman pushed her way through the crowd and came up close to the glass. Her eyes met his, blazing and hot. She yelled something he couldn't make out, the same word over and over. Then she slammed a piece of paper up against the glass, the picture of Rachel that Walford had shown him earlier. The thing she was yelling, she started to yell harder.

His mother sobbed, yelling something different. An officer pushed his way from the back of the crowd and wedged between the women.

Dr. Graham reached Walford and punched him hard on the jaw. The punch sent Walford stumbling into the wall, crashing to the floor.

"If we don't follow the protocol—"

"I don't care about your protocol. Graciela, do it. *Do it.*"

"What the—"

Dr. Graham turned to Graciela, now standing beside a complicated piece of equipment. Several screens. A bank of buttons. Wires that snaked from its sides over to Andrew. Graciela had been silent during the chaos, not moving. She caught his eye.

"Ramon Caldevera was my stepson. Nine bullets. *Nine.* He was fifteen. I hope you burn in Hell."

Graciela hit a button on the machine's bank, and it lit up a bright green. Dr. Graham yelled something, but Andrew couldn't quite hear it. The hot burst of light came again, but this one set his body on fire. Every nerve came alive; he could feel everything, and everything burned. The five bullets burned particularly bright.

He was in the school again, standing over Rachel, only this time she was awake, eyes open, terrified. She looked up at him, arms stretched out in front of her.

"Please, Andrew, please don't. Please. Please."

"Oh, now you notice me, bitch." It was his voice. "Too late. Game over."

Pop pop pop pop from the gun in his hand, and Rachel screamed. Her body convulsed from the force of the bullets, sobbing and choking on the blood welling up in her throat where he'd shot her.

He was now in the hallway, facing Reynold. This time he wasn't nostalgic, he was filled with hate. "You forgot me!" His voice was echoing in the hallway. "*You* forgot *me.*" The hate was mixed with shame. "Fuck you, asshole." *Pop pop pop pop pop.* Reynold was dead.

He saw every person he killed, one by one, including Ramon Caldevera, shot nine times because he was stupid enough to try to hide in the bathroom. The fire in his body matched the fire in his mind.

He was in the office again, hunkered down, assault rifle held close at the ready, hearing the footsteps outside the door. *Now, they'll remember me.* The footsteps got closer. *They'll always be scared of the noise behind them, wherever they are.* The door swung open. *They'll always be afraid. I will live forever.* The police officer entered the room and he stood with his weapon. He aimed at the officer, and let out a yell. *Pop pop pop pop pop.* Five bullets finding their home. The fire across his body. Then haze. Then black.

He was back in the revitalization room, which had descended into chaos. The people behind the glass, the families of the people he'd killed, were yelling at him, slamming their fists on the glass, pushing forward in silent rage.

He smiled. They looked like little gerbils in the cages at a pet store. Stupid, frightened, clueless.

Dr. Graham was back, yelling something at Graciela, who was crying and spitting words back at him.

"It's done." Dr. Graham's voice barely contained his anger. "I don't care about their money. I should never have agreed this."

He pushed Graciela out of the way and held his hand over the last button on the bank of the machine.

"It wasn't enough that you were dead." His voice was tired. "They needed to see it. They used their savings, everything they had, all of them. They needed to see it."

"I'd kill them, too."

"They just should have been glad you were dead."

Dr. Graham pushed the button. New things were moving through Andrew's blood, cooling the fire until it was more like ice.

The people behind the glass had calmed. His mother was still sobbing. Unable to look. Rachel's mother was mouthing the words from before, and he could finally make them out: *murderer murderer murderer murderer.*

The bullet beneath his left eye twisted in the muscle. *You'll always be scared and I will live forever.* The world began to go black again. *You'll always be scared and I will live forever.*

Monstrous Practices

P.C. Keeler

"CODE SHAVE!" BLARED THE OVERHEAD speakers. "Orderlies, please report to long-term care. Code Shave! Orderlies, please report to long-term care."

Charlie looked around the waiting room to see if anyone would go running through, but nothing happened. The receptionists were typing at their desks, all the other patients were sitting in their stinky plastic seats, and the TV was still showing news about an old bridge getting blown up now that the new, better bridge was open. But it wasn't going to actually blow up until tomorrow, so even explosions failed him. The hospital so far wasn't any more exciting than being back with the rest of the second-graders.

Charlie looked down at his leg. That was still sort of exciting. There was a thick cardboard support around the whole leg, keeping it straight and propped up on a stool someone had brought over. There were lots of bruises and cuts all around his knee, and the shin still wasn't quite straight under the skin. It had been a really bad fall. He still thought he could jump across that culvert if he had another try. Once his leg was fixed.

Vice-Principal Leslie patted Charlie on his back. "Your mom will be here soon, Charlie," she said. "Are you feeling all right? Does it still hurt?" Vice-Principal Leslie had been at Nando Elementary for two hundred years and had blue hair on one side and tight black curls on the other. She had a big bolt on either side of her neck and this year her face had a pointy chin and round nose and two skinny eyebrows she waggled when she was being funny. She'd come to the hospital with him because Mrs. Marcy had to stay with the class.

Charlie shook his head. "No, Miss Leslie," he said truthfully. It had hurt a whole lot when it happened, yeah. And he'd been crying while they waited for the ambulance, and when they got the board underneath him and lifted him into the back. But then once he was out of the sun, the very pale driver came into the back, carefully staying away from the light, and looked him right in the eyes and said, "Don't move. It doesn't hurt anymore." Then the driver waited a minute and said, "Does it hurt now?"

Looking into the driver's eyes was weird, like anything he said would be right. Charlie had stayed very still and said, "No, it doesn't hurt." Because now it didn't, just like the driver said.

Then the driver gave him a sharp, toothy smile with two big fangs and said, "Good boy." Then they drove to the hospital while the other EMT people got Charlie's leg straightened out and into the temporary cast.

Now, Charlie was staying very still in the waiting room, and it still didn't hurt. He could feel that his leg was really messed up, but it didn't hurt. So he was just bored.

"Once your mom gets here, she can give them permission to get you all fixed up," Vice-Principal Leslie told him. "Until then, it's still a school day, so we should have a lesson."

Charlie wanted to let out a really big sigh. He wasn't *at* school, so he shouldn't have to *have* school. That seemed like the most totally obvious thing in the world to him. But Vice-Principal Leslie was in charge of the teachers, so of course she would think she had to do teaching. So, "Yes, Miss Leslie," he said.

She patted him on the shoulder with a hand that had most of a dolphin tattoo on the wrist, until it ran into the stitches, and then the arm above that was a different color. "Do you know how people used to do medicine in the old days?" she asked.

Charlie nodded. He'd read a book about that. "They put needles in people and cut them apart and then took all their money."

Miss Leslie laughed. "That's a good starting point. It was expensive because they had to be very, very careful about how they cut into people, yes. It took years to learn to become a doctor. There still are some people who go to all that work today. Some of them take the time because there are still important things to research and they need to learn an awful lot first. But others become doctors that way because some people don't like modern medicine, which is called *lykotic treatment*."

105

Charlie thought about that. He didn't like modern medicine, either. It was really boring, so far. There was a lot of sitting still and not doing anything. But it was better than having someone cut his leg up. "Why don't they like it?"

That big hand with most of a dolphin tattoo patted his shoulder again. "Well, Charlie, some people don't think anyone should use modern medicine, and should go back to the old way. Some say that traditional medicine might not work as well, but they understand it better, so they trust it more. There's a thing all people in medicine have to promise, called the *Hippocratic Oath*, which says a lot of things, but mostly it says 'I will make people better.' The people who don't like modern medicine are refusing to do things that make people better, so they're called *Hippocrites*. That's a pun, because the word 'hypocrites' means people who say one thing and do another."

Charlie liked that word. Hippocrites. It sounded like that blue bird from *The Lion King* telling all the hippos that they were hippo-ing wrong. "No, no, no! You float *that* way!" But Miss Leslie was still teaching and looking right at him, so he had to keep listening.

"Most people prefer normal treatment. It's very easy and it works on almost any kind of injury, like yours. There's a special nurse who can turn into a wolf any time the moon is full. She has training so she can change just a little bit if she wants to, and share that ability with other people. The nurse will give you a little nip on the arm, and then you'll wait in a room called a *lunarium* while you go through what's called the *change*. Basically, your body will shift itself into a new shape and fix all the damage along the way. Then we take you out of the lunarium, give you the antidote, the change will revert in a few minutes, and you'll be all better. If you had some kind of long-term problem, then you might have to come to the hospital regularly for treatment, but you just have a broken leg."

Charlie looked down at his leg again. The ambulance driver with the big fangs had said to not move and so he still wasn't moving, but he could look around. "Who has to come to the hospital regularly?"

Miss Leslie patted his shoulder. "Mostly only people with what are called genetic diseases. Their bodies don't always work quite right on their own, so they have to come get fixed up every few months, or even days. But people who have those kinds of conditions know about it very early, so if you haven't found any genetic diseases before now, you don't have any. You might have met several other kids who have genetic diseases, and thanks to modern medicine, you couldn't even tell that they need help to keep their muscles and lungs working right."

Charlie thought a moment. "Why didn't I come to the hospital to get better when I had a cold?"

Miss Leslie smiled. She was always nice. "The change can fix damage to your body, but it can't actually cure diseases. Sometimes, that feeling of being sick is your body fighting off the germs that are trying to infect you. If you fixed all the ways you feel bad, it would actually keep you from getting better, because the germs would still be there. That's one of the reasons some people still do learn the old kind of medicine, because figuring out sicknesses is one thing that kind of medicine does very well, even today."

"Why didn't everyone just use the new medicine to start?" Charlie asked.

"Well, the new medicine actually was thought of as a disease itself for a very long time. Not only that, people were afraid of the change. If they saw someone who had changed, they would chase them away or hurt them. It can be a little scary to watch. Someone going through the change gets sharp fangs and claws, hair all over, and a tail. Only until it wears off, of course. Then we give you the antidote and you don't have to worry about it again. As long as you don't go jumping over any more culverts!"

Charlie's eyes lit up. "And somebody who doesn't get the antidote is a Code Shave, so they can get the hair back off!"

Vice-Principal Leslie laughed. "Very good, Charlie! Look, there's your mom. She needs to sign a form, and then we'll get you healed right up. Tomorrow you can tell your classmates all about it."

"Can I come in with claws and fangs and a tail?"

"Sorry, Charlie. The hospital won't let you go until you take the antidote. People tend to be a little rowdy while they're in the change."

Furry Little Things on a Full Moon Night

Excerpt from: *Hairwolf*

D.J. Whitney

"...WHERE ARE YOU?"

"I'm on the back porch looking for Ben Herr. Come on, kitty, kitty..."

"Come on, kitty, kitty."

Tucked within her wool-lined, denim jacket, ten-year-old Stef stands transfixed on something strange out in the wheat fields. It's early evening and what holds her gaze is silhouetted by the full moon cresting the horizon. She's waiting for her eyes to adjust to the darkness to identify what it is. Out here, there're no houses. No city lights. This is farm land, Arkansas.

The landscape is flat and offers an unimpeded view to the horizon. If it wasn't for the moonlight, she'd be staring into complete darkness. But the fact that this thing is backlit by the moon isn't helping her, either.

"Can't be a fence post. I'd remember a fence post out here. But then again, maybe not. I don't always remember the everyday things I see—every day. Why does it look like you're looking back at me?"

She tries adjusting her vantage point from the porch to make sense of this enigma, but it doesn't help. She can make out a crown between what appears to be two ears, but there's a piece missing from the tip of the left ear. "That's odd." As her eyes adjust to the darkness, more and more details begin to stand out. She can clearly see the outline of a head and a very thick neck sitting on top of some very broad shoulders.

"If it wasn't for that odd-shaped ear, you could be really real. What are you? Oh! I'll bet Ralf put the scarecrow up without me." She looks over to the side of the house where the scarecrow is leaning. "Nope. It's not the scarecrow." She waves at it. "Any day now, scarecrow. Be patient." She turns back to her mystery figure, realizing, "Oh, duh! You're a shadow-made! Oh, man, you really had me going there. Good job!"

She pulls her hair out from under her coat and flips up her collar, feeling a slight chill. Her eyes land on her shadow-made once again. That's no surprise. They're usually right where you left them, providing the shadow hasn't changed. "I'll be seeing you in the daytime."

From inside, ten-year-old Ralf sarcastically remarks, "If

you want the cat, it'd help if you called him."

"Hey, Ralf," Stef replies. "I made a shadow-made in your field. I'm going to call it Ominous. It's really cool."

"I'd get up and look, but I'm busy working on your necklace. You know—the one I asked you to help me with?"

"You still need my help?"

"Not now."

"I'll be right in. I want to see if I can make another shadow-made. Where are you, Ben? Kitty, kitty."

She searches for more oddities, but nothing is standing out like her Ominous. She swats at the mosquitoes buzzing her, vying for her blood. But she won't give up easily. Then the unimaginable happens. Her shadow-made moves, and it's not supposed to. It's getting lower in the field, as if trying to hide. At least that's what it looks like. It's not as tall as it was moments earlier.

"What the . . . ?" She's up on her tippy toes, trying to keep an eye on it, but it disappears into the grass.

"Oh, no, you didn't!" She bounces down the rear steps into the backyard. She's more stubborn than cautious. She marches through the tall grass, sweeping away the sharp blades. This is familiar territory for her. She and Ralf play here all the time. She looks for a slight rise in the field. Reaching its apex, she searches for her shadow-made.

Then, just as slowly as her shadow-made dipped into the grass, it rises back up. Only now it's several yards away. She pauses. Now the two are nearly face to face. As the moon falls behind a cloud, she struggles to see clearly in the darkness. One thing is clear: he's not moving, and neither is she. Not so much because she's frightened, which she isn't. She's a tough and curious girl. No, it's because she's stubborn. She's going to watch this thing and figure out what the heck it is. There has to be a logical explanation for why it moved. But what?

This one is going to be tricky to figure out. Shadow-mades don't move. Cloud-mades move. They're supposed to. They're clouds. Maybe she should call Ralf? He lives here. It's his family's farm. She plays here with him, but he knows this place better than she does. He'd love this one.

But then he wouldn't let her live it down. No. She's got to figure this one out on her own.

An uneasy feeling washes over her, raising the tiny hairs on her neck and arms. She sweeps her hand over her arms with a shiver. She knows this feeling. The teachers speak of it all the time in school. It's called leaving one's comfort zone.

But this is her field. Hers and Ralf's. Not the shadow-made's.

"This is ridiculous," she tells herself. "Come on, Stef. It's a shadow-made. What's it going to do? All right. Gonna go now. Here we go. One small step for Schteffy girl, one large step for . . ."

"*Meow!*" cries Ben Herr, catching Stef's foot on the back of his tail.

Both he and Stef jump from fear. Stef laughs and scolds, "You scared the heck out of me, Ben."

Ben Herr races out of the grass with Stef close behind. "I'll bet you were just waiting to get me, weren't you? Come here, kitty. Are you okay? Did I hurt you?"

He waits for her on the steps. She takes a seat next to him and hugs him. He wants to go inside. Stef stands at the top of the stairs looking out into the darkness for her shadow-made. There it is, higher in the grass and looking back at her. Now she's really perplexed. Border-lining-mad perplexed. It's one thing to be spooked by a shadow-made, but quite another to be outsmarted by one. She knows it's just a figment of her imagination. But this guy, her Ominous, seems to have a figment of its own imagination. And that would be a first, at least regarding all of her shadow-made experiences, which are usually revealed when the lights come on or her eyes adjust to the dark. And that could be what's going on here. There's too much waffling moonlight and not enough time for her eyes to properly adjust.

"Sorry, Ominous. I'm not falling for that again. You had your chance."

Abigail, Ralf's mom, steps onto the porch from the house wearing a pullover apron. She's a woman of thirty, farm-worn and healthy. Ralf follows behind her, pausing at the door to scratch his back on the door frame. He's a large boy for ten, and cute as a button with red hair.

"Who you talking to, Stef?" asks Abigail.

"My shadow-made. See it? It's . . . Not again. It was right there. In the field. I'll bet it's the moonlight. It's changing the shadows."

"There you go. Blame the moon," Ralf says. "You're the one acting like a lunatic, and it's the moon's fault."

Both Abigail and Stef stare at him, blank-faced.

"Eh, eh! Get it?" he quips. "Luna-tick." He returns to the inside with, "There'll be another show at seven. Bring the kids and someone to explain the humor." He stops at the door for another scratch.

"What humor?" asks Stef.

Abigail laughs out loud. They high-five.

They follow Ralf back into the house, watching him try to reach his upper back.

113

"Damn it," he complains, as he takes a seat at the kitchen table. "Hey, Stef, see what's back there. It's itching me to death."

Stef crosses behind his chair as Abigail enters the bathroom just outside the kitchen. Stef pulls down his shirt collar and notices several strands of long hair retreating back into his skin. "Whoa," she says, alarmed.

"What? What is it? A bug?"

"Your hair is alive. It just crawled back into your skin. Did you do that?"

"From now on, leave the humor to me." Ralf picks up his needle-nose pliers and continues working on the chain links of her necklace.

"Don't believe me! But if I were you, I'd get the name of a barber that makes house-calls. You're going to need it." Looking at the necklace, she comments, "Good job, Ralf."

Stef opens the door for Ben Herr and takes another look for her shadow-made. It's gone. Very, very strange.

"You know, I could make this into a bracelet."

She turns to him, noticing he's looking through the links of her chain, ready to snip them in half with the pliers . . .

"No, don't," she yells, advancing on him.

Ralf is surprised at her reaction and lowers the necklace and pliers. "I'm only kidding. I wouldn't carve up your necklace."

Abigail enters the kitchen.

"Look at her, Mom."

Stef drops down in her chair, feeling very foolish. Abigail crosses to her.

"You okay, sweetie? That's your mother's necklace, isn't it?" asks Abigail.

Stef nods.

Ralf had no idea. "Your real mom? I thought it was your foster mom's. Oh, this is going to cost you," he says. "Give me a little heads-up next time, will ya?"

"There won't be a next time. That's all I have. There isn't anything else."

"This is all she left you?" he asks.

"They were in a hurry," she says. "At least, that's what I was told by my foster parents."

Ralf doesn't like that at all. How could any parent abandon their only child—any child—without saying goodbye? "Mom, if you ever abandon me, leave the keys to the truck and a couple of grand. You can keep the jewelry."

Abigail hopes he hasn't said that. But he did. And it's out there. Fortunately, Stef is laughing.

A short time later, dinner is served. Stef watches with total disgust as Ralf chews on a strange piece of meat. Her fork has several green beans stuck in the prongs, waiting to be eaten. There's not one piece of meat on her plate or one piece of veggie on his. Unless one considers a tomato a veggie.

"Want a bite?" he asks, baiting her. "It's good. Better when you stalk it, shoot it, and skin it."

"Poor little bunny," Stef whispers. "Never had a chance."

"He's really quite the game hunter, isn't he, Stef?" asks Abigail.

Ralf can't believe the betrayal from his mom. She smiles it off.

"Where you going to mount the head?" Stef asks, sarcastically. "Over your fireplace, next to your dad's moose head? Little tiny bunny next to a giant moose. You'll need glasses just to be able to see it."

"Tell ya where I'm gonna mount it, you keep this up."

"Ralf . . ." Abigail protests, laughing.

Ralf is suddenly stricken with a sharp pain in his stomach. Abigail and Stef notice. "Ralf . . . are you okay, honey?"

"My stomach," he says, grimacing in pain.

"Do you think it's the rabbit?" asks Stef.

"No. Food poisoning takes at least twelve hours," he says, trying to push his plate aside. The pain keeps his arms tight to his stomach. He tries to fight back the pain, but the pain is winning. And then suddenly, it's gone. The pain is gone. He breathes in slowly and deeply, as if testing. But it's gone. "Whew! It's gone. I knew I should have farted when I had the chance."

Abigail slaps the table in protest . . . "You did not just say that!"

Stef is grossed out over the thought of that happening, especially at the dinner table. But she has another concern. It's the uneaten bunny meat.

"You're still going to eat that, right? You have to eat it. You told me you have to respect the spirit of the animal by eating it after you killed it. Maybe that's why you have the pain."

"Relax! I'll eat it tomorrow. Ready, Stef? Try on your new necklace?"

Ralf rises from the table with Stefanie's necklace, an Egyptian ankh. He walks behind her as she lifts up her hair. He places it around her neck and clasps it. It falls just shy of her neckline. "Thanks, Ralf."

"I shortened it and attached the spare chain-links to the sides of the medallion. As you get older and grow boobs, we can lengthen the chain."

"You—really, Ralf?" Abigail says, leaving Stef at a complete loss for words. She notices Stef holding the ankh, fighting back tears. Abigail gestures to Ralf. He leans over Stef's shoulder and pulls a tear from her cheek with his finger.

"Hey . . ." he says gently. "You okay? You have us, you know? We'll find them someday. Then you can ask why they left."

Stef looks up at Abigail, who's biting her tongue. Abigail knows something, but what? She sits down next to Stef.

"I know your parents loved you very much. But they had to leave. They had no choice. It was the hardest thing ever for them. Someday, you'll understand."

"I want to understand now."

"So do I, sweetie. So do I."

Ralf and Stef walk along the paved road bordered by tall fields of grass. A single streetlight shines down over a crossroad just ahead. In the fields, fireflies illuminate the blanket of moisture lying across the tall grasses. Stef runs off into the fields, chasing after the fireflies. She gestures for Ralf to follow. He does, but ever so slowly. His stomach appears to be acting up again. She races back to him. "What's the matter?"

"My stomach again."

Suddenly, a loud hissing escapes from the fields. It's coming from all around, surrounding them. Ralf pulls her in close to his side, ready to protect her. He looks for the source of the hissing through the darkness, cautious and concerned. He's ready to take on whatever it is, ready to protect her, or at least try. It's frightening, as well as loud. But Stef is unmoved.

Again, she's more curious than cautious. She's nearly tippy-toed, vying for higher ground to find the source.

He gestures to Stef. "Don't move!"

"I want to know what it is."

"No, you don't!" he says, as if knowing something she doesn't. But it goes unnoticed, due to her curiosity of what's lurking out there.

"Yes, I do!"

Waiting, watching the darkness, the hissing spits and sputters. Then powerful jets of water shoot out from various nozzles of a large sprinkler system.

"Goddamn it!" Ralf proclaims. "Friggin' sprinklers. Scared the hell out of me. Shit, shit, and shit!"

Stef screams with laughter and races out of the field, dodging all the sprinkler jets. Ralf runs after her, but much slower. He enters the road, drenched. Stef looks at him, elated. These are good times for her. Fun times. Not so much for Ralf, though. He's got stomach cramps and is wet from head to toe. She removes her coat and wipes his hair and face dry. He stands there, letting her.

"What'd you do, aim for every single sprinkler jet?"

"Apparently." He needs to sit down. The stomach pain is intensifying.

Stef sits next to him, concerned. "Is it really gas?"

"I don't know," he says, fighting back the pain. "I thought it was. Maybe I sprained a stomach muscle."

"Let me get your mom."

"No! I just need a minute."

"Come on. I'll walk you back home," she offers. But he doesn't want her to do that. He's really at a loss. He'd like to just stay there for the rest of the night. The pain is that bad.

"Go back home, Ralf. I'll be fine. I'll call when I get home."

He looks around into the dark night. He doesn't like the idea, but he's in no shape to continue on.

"I'll cut through the field and call you as soon as I get home. But you gotta go back now. Go on!"

"Let me wait here a few minutes. Go ahead. I'll watch you," he says.

"Okay. There're more fireflies over the fields, anyway." She offers, "They'll keep me company. See you tomorrow."

Stef walks off, looking back on him frequently. As she approaches the tractor trail, she turns to wave, but he's gone. She struggles to see him, but can't. "That was fast."

She enters the tractor trail through the field. She likes this path. It's like the Yellow Brick Road to her. The grass between the worn tire tracks is lower than the surrounding tall grass. The road is dotted with exposed boulders and rocks. It's very inviting. She stays on the right side because it's higher than the left and allows her to see over the fields.

Soon she'll be home and calling Ralf. As she tracks along, the fireflies light up her path. Not that she needs it. The light from the moon is doing a fine job of that. She hums along with the choir of crickets until she's the only one humming. Then suddenly, all the fireflies and crickets disappear.

She becomes alert, cautious. This could mean predator. Maybe a coyote or a bobcat.

Something scared off all the insects. The hairs on her arm rise and she sweeps her hand over them, curious. As much as she'd love to see one, she knows they could be dangerous. She'll be very quiet from this point on.

She stops and listens. All she can hear is the soft breeze

blowing through the tops of the tall grass. It's comforting, but the fact that it's the only sound out here is troubling. Then she hears the trampling of something very large running and stopping through the field as if it's on the hunt for something.

She proceeds cautiously, as does the rumbling. The sounds that this thing is making are too large to be a bobcat or a coyote. Maybe it's Ralf. Maybe he's playing a trick on her. She whispers, "Ralf? Is that you?" There's no response. She smells something foul in the air. It's familiar to her but she can't remember what it is. She looks ahead into the dark and walks faster and faster towards an abandoned, rack-body truck. She senses something is following her. She doesn't know how she knows. She just does. Much like the comfort-zone awareness cues she learned in school, she doesn't understand them either, but she knows when they're present. And her senses are telling her whatever it is that's following her is getting closer to finding her.

"Please stop! You need to stop," she says. She runs to the truck and grabs the passenger door handle. Hopefully, it's Ralf playing games with her. But what if it isn't?

She listens but it's hard to hear over her own breathing. She holds her breath, eyes scanning the fields, listening sharply. But there's only the sound of her beating heart—which is very loud at the moment. She doesn't hear anything else.

She releases the door handle and starts on her way. But the noise starts up again. It's weird, unsettling. As soon as she moves, she hears the disturbance. As soon as she stops, whatever this thing is, whoever it is, stops as well. And it has to be big. It's moving a lot of grass all at once. It's also unyielding in the darkness. If it were small, it'd be careful, cautious, yielding to predators. But it's not. It's as if this thing is the sole predator out here and doesn't care who knows it's here. Maybe it's a bear? She has to hide. She returns to the truck.

She pushes down on the chrome button, but it's rusted stuck. She places her left hand over her right thumb and presses down with all her might. It clicks loudly, echoing in the darkness and across the fields. She listens but doesn't hear it anymore. Now, she's getting mad.

She pulls the door open slowly. The years of rust cause it to crick and crack like fireworks in the dead of night. She pauses, trying to hush the noise. As she does, she hears the creature racing through the grass straight at her. It's getting louder and closer right towards her. Its pace has picked up.

She swings the door open and scrambles into the cobweb-covered cab. The webs lace across her face but she ignores them. She scrambles for cover on the dark floorboards.

As she sweeps the cobwebs from her face, she reaches up for the door handle and pulls it closed.

She's in and the door is closed. She tucks down on the floorboard, waiting, listening. Then she realizes she didn't lock the door. She slaps at the locking pin.

She skips a breath, trying to capture a sound here and there, but everything outside is muffled.

Stef stretches over to the driver's door and swats at the lock pin. She then notices both windows are opened about an inch and the handles are missing. She withdraws back under the dash, thoughts racing on what to do. There's nothing she can do. She reaches for her ankh necklace, being the last harbor of security she has—the one and only thing left to her from her real mother. But it's gone. "Where is it? Oh, no!"

She palms the floorboard with her fingertips, searching for it, but it's not there. She checks her shirt frantically, then her hair and the floor again, but she can't find it. She rethinks her steps. She knows it can't be far. But with this thing being out there, she can't go outside and look for it. She's getting mad. Mad might be a better emotion right now. Mad would give her more control than what fear is giving her. Fear is making her feel like prey. And she isn't prey.

Whatever this thing is that's holding her hostage wants something. But what? And why her?

Just then, a large, dark shadow sweeps across the window. Now she knows it's just outside. She can hear it breathing through the tiny opening in the passenger window. But its breathing is different than anything she's ever heard. There's a lot of power pushing out this breath, indicating it to be very, very large. She freezes, unsure what to do. Then she hears growling.

She rises slowly to see what it is. *Crash*. The truck rocks violently back and forth. She braces herself under the dashboard, waiting for it to end. She glances out the rear window and sees something very large and very thick, deliberately rocking the truck back and forth. It has a human form but it's too big to be Ralf. What is this thing? Its weight is causing the truck to bottom out on the suspension. She tucks up in the shadows, keeping as much of herself out of sight as possible. Maybe it won't see her? Maybe it will just go away?

Stef, shaking from fear, can feel her heart pound through her chest. The rocking stops. She steals a peek out the rear window.

The full moon fills a corner, allowing her to see the outline of the creature's silhouette. It's eerily a lot like her shadow-made. The shape, the broad shoulders, the thick neck. As she looks closer, she notices the ruff on its head. It also looks male. Of this, she's sure. Whatever this thing is, it's male. But then she notices something awful. Something very, very frightening. She notices his left ear is missing a piece of flesh right at the tip, just like her shadow made. This is impossible. How did this happen? As he faces the moon, she gets a better look at him. He's unlike anything she's ever seen.

He has a face full of fur and muscles that are ripping his shirt. It's definitely her shadow-made, Ominous. And he's really real. Ominous leaps from the truck, rocking it back and forth, and lands outside the passenger door.

Stef panics. She cowers down even more than before, tucking herself under the dash as far as she can. Her head is pinned between her knees, eyes closed. Her breathing is getting louder and louder. Suddenly, she realizes the breathing isn't hers. She cranes her head slowly up at the passenger window. She can't see anything. Maybe he's gone. She inches out farther and freezes. He isn't gone. His entire frame is blocking out the window. And what's worse, her movement has captured his attention and he's looking back at her. He's close. Too close.

He looks like a man, but isn't. Men aren't covered with fur. He looks like an animal, but isn't. Animals don't wear clothes. What is this thing? What is he? Then her worst fears are realized. He howls, long and loud, elated over his find. He sounds just like a wolf. But isn't, which could only mean one thing. Her shadow-made is a werewolf.

Glistening in the light and protruding from the corners of his mouth are long fangs, dripping with drool. She didn't see that before. She didn't see a lot of this before. She watches as he raises his long, black claws up to the glass, tapping at it, scratching at it, as if curious of its consistency. The claws glisten in the brilliant moonlight. He slides the tips of his claws down the glass, unfamiliar with the material, possibly due to his current state of being. And he wants this little girl.

Stretching across his brow is a thin, dark band of fur, which looks like a mask. But it's no mask. The bottom of his nose is shiny, like leather, much like that of a canine. Fur covers a large portion of his face, but then there are patches of skin, such as on his cheekbones.

He sniffs the air for her scent, but it's vague. He's intrigued at the sight of her but wants more. He wants her. He studies the clear material dividing them. There has to be a way in. His claws are searching for an entry point. He has yet to notice the window cracked down slightly, but he will. It's only a matter of time. She needs to do something.

He starts tapping at the glass with his long, black, pointed claws, testing its strength. She's right there, just beyond the thin, invisible barrier. Now, if he could get through it.

He howls. She screams. He likes that. He howls again. She screams again. The nightmare for her is real, but to him, it's play. Playtime with his prey.

She can't look away, but can't look at him, either. She's trapped and has no way out. His constant tapping at the glass sends chills through her body. She's getting mad. "Stop it! Go away! Leave me alone!"

He claws frantically at the window, wanting to get in. Needing to get in.

Stef screams hysterically, "Go away! Get away from me! Help! Somebody, help! Get away!"

"Somebody, help! Get away!"

From somewhere, a woman's voice calls out to her, frantically—"That's it! On the count of three, you'll be here with me. One. Coming back now, Stef. Two, almost here . . ."

Flashes of light punch through the darkness of the cab, erasing the present into the past. Current images morph into the present . . . the floorboard becomes a room. The window, decorative walls. The moon, a faulty ceiling light fluttering above. Darkness fades as the voice summons her . . .

". . . And three. You're back with me. Stefanie? Can you hear me?"

Stef jumps from the couch, kicking and ready to run. Lillian, agile and strong, grabs her and settles her back, gently and reassuringly.

It's present day, thirty years later. Stef, wet with sweat, sways, disorientated. Her long, dirty blonde hair sticks to her wet face. She steadies herself, reaching for the back of a chair as the safety and security of her current reality seeps in.

"You're okay, Stef. You're with me," says Lillian.

Stef drops back down, recapturing the events, playing them back up to the point of extraction. But instead of feeling relief or safety, Stef throws her arms out in frustration.

"Damn it!"

Lillian finds her reaction a little inconsistent, considering what she just revealed. "Damn it? Don't you mean 'Holy shit?' Or 'What the frig was that?' 'Damn it' is for stubbing a toe, not getting your ass kicked by some freak-show fangster."

"What did you do?" Stef asks, somewhat accusatory. "Why did you pull me out?"

"You were about to be attacked. What'd you want me to do? Leave you in there? You didn't prepare me for that. I have to be prepared for something like that."

"I asked you not to pull me out—no matter what."

Lillian rises. "Then you should have told me what to expect. Jesus H. Christ! What the hell was that thing!? What was it?" Lillian waits for an answer, but it isn't coming. Stef is frustrated and paces back and forth. Lillian complains, "Like a goddamn horror movie. Of course I pulled you out. What was that thing?"

"I know what it was. What I need to know is *who* it was."

"Listen to yourself."

Stef's really disappointed with the failure of the session. She wanted answers and that's not what she got. Suddenly, it dawns on Lillian what this is really about . . .

"Oh, Stef. Oh, no. Stef . . . honey . . . I'm so sorry. I didn't even think about . . ."

"What?" Stef asks. But then, realizing where Lillian is going, she defends herself. "No! That's . . . wrong diagnosis, Lillian."

"You're ten years old, chased by someone you knew and most likely trusted, and they attack you in a pickup truck."

"I wasn't attacked. I mean, I was, but not in that sense. And it was a rack body," Stef says while taking a moment to regroup.

"Rack . . . what?"

"It wasn't a pickup. It was a rack body. A flatbed with wooden racks."

Lillian considers her with serious doubt, commenting, "You remember that, but not who it was? Oh, honey, this is so textbook. I have chapters covering events like this in my lesson books."

"You don't have lessons for this," Stef says adamantly.

Lillian leans back, knowing who's right here. Stef can deny all she wants, but Lillian knows the truth.

"Stop it, Lillian! I know what you're thinking." Stef takes her bag and jacket from the chair and heads towards the door with, "I have to go." She's very disappointed, not to mention exhausted.

"You can run, but you can't hide," advises Lillian.

"I'm not running or hiding. I'm going home to pack, and then I'm going to work. And you can wipe that 'you know what's wrong with me because you're a therapist' look off of your face. I'll be off Monday. Let me know when we could do this again, without pulling me out of the session."

"Oh, no. I ain't doing that shit again. Not without a specialist by my side. I can't. I won't! I'm not qualified."

Stef closes the door and crosses back to Lillian, following her to her desk and her address book. Lillian fingers the pages. "I know someone. She owes me big time. It'll be our secret, and on the house."

"Will you stop with this! I wasn't raped. I let you hypnotize me because we're friends – and you owed me fifty bucks. I figured, what the hell, maybe I'll find something out. And I almost did. Lillian, I can't go to anyone else. You're the only person I trust. You have to do this for me. If you don't, I'll never find out. I need to know who he was and who else was there."

Lillian considers her plea. Her sincerity. But it really makes no sense at all to her. "Hear me out," Lillian offers. "First scenario, your parents adopted you when you were five, right? You yourself said there was never a parent-child connection, but you loved them regardless. Something happened, once, maybe more, who knows? But it was so horribly tragic that the only way for you to cope with it was to make that man into a monster. But you're saying no, you weren't raped. Which leaves us with scenario number two: you were attacked by a friggin' werewolf and you want to know who he was. The fact that you were attacked doesn't bother you. The fact that you turned him into a werewolf doesn't bother you. What bothers you is not knowing who he is. See where I'm going with this?"

"I never said he was a werewolf."

"Really? An animal dressed like a man that howls . . . sounds like a werewolf to me. What do you want to call it?"

"Lillian, please. I need your help."

"I'll give you one more session. On one condition. You tell me why, and I want the truth."

"Thank you. I'll tell you before the session, I promise. I have to go. Love you."

"Love you back."

Stef gives her a hug and races out the door.

Lillian plops down in her chair, considering a photo of Stef and her taken years ago on her mantle. They're eating large cotton candies.

To think that Stef has been harboring this attack for so long pains her. She knows what she knows and feels for Stef. Lillian's beside herself on how to help her. "Ten years old. My God in Heaven. No wonder she avoids relationships. She doesn't trust anybody—except me. She trusts me! I'm all the family she has. You got to be on top of your game for this one, Lillian." She goes to a shelf, retrieving a book on traumas. She opens to a bookmark on child abuse and starts reading. After a second, she stops. Her shoulders drop as she realizes the saddest part of all of this is that she has a bookmark on the subject.

Stef is seated at a dinner table at the house of Mr. Winster. He's an eighty-something-year-old man she takes care of on the weekends. He exits his bedroom with a pair of hiking knives and sets them down on the table. He takes a seat across from her.

"You still have them?" Stef says. "I thought you gave them away. I was going to ask if I could buy them."

"I was saving these for my grandkids," he says, pulling the larger of the two bowie knives from its leather sheath. "But, boy, what a disappointment they turned out to be. The only time they're outside is walking to the car. Never go outdoors and play. No, these are for you. A gift. Put 'em to use. They've been sitting in my drawer way too long."

Stef pulls the set over to her side of the table with, "Done! What else you got?"

Winster, expecting maybe something a little different, sits with mouth agape. But she's unable to keep a straight face, and . . .

"I'm only kidding. You have no idea how much this means to me. Actually, you do. And you're probably the only one. You know I'm going to use them. I thought you gave them away or sold them or something. Why don't you keep them out anymore?"

"Because seeing them only reminds me of the things I can't do anymore. I'm no longer able to go off into the woods for hours at a time. And when I see those knives, it's just something else I don't need to be reminded of."

She didn't think of that.

"I'm fine with getting old," he adds. "But it does take some getting used to. I need to create new things I can do to help forget the ones I can't."

"Few things about my life I'm trying to forget."

"Like what?"

"Childhood."

"What part of your childhood are you trying to forget?" he asks, puzzled.

"The childhood part," she offers casually, holding one of the knives in her hand, testing the feel and fit. She notices his bewilderment over the comment.

"My parents left me when I was five," she offers. "I was fostered out to a family that needed a totem child to keep them together."

He's waiting for more. She didn't quite answer him and she's not really sure she wants to.

"The part I'm trying to forget is remembering that I was abandoned. Why would anyone do that to a child?" she says. "Why wait that long to unload them? Do it right off of the bat or don't have them at all. Shit! It's not a very good confidence builder. You know?"

"You don't know why they left?" he asks.

"No."

"Bad parenting aside, you're who you are today because of it, so embrace it," he says, matter-of-factly.

"Embrace it? That's a pretty harsh thing to say," she says. " 'Suck it up, Stef. Your parents left you. Shit happens, get over it.' "

"I didn't mean it like that. There're some things we just can't change. But what we can change is how they affect us." He continues, "Childhood memories help us know who we are."

"I was orphaned. Therefore I'm an orphan. That's what I am. How does that help me?"

"What if . . . what if that was what you agreed to? What if, somehow, you and—God, for argument's sake—got together before you were born and decided this would be one of the lessons you would learn? Would you feel less the victim?"

"Why would anybody choose something like that?"

"Would you feel less the victim?" he repeats in a forceful tone, demanding an answer.

"If I agreed to those circumstances? Yes, I'd feel less the victim but more a moron, knowing I was the dumbass that agreed to it."

"Okay, good. So what lessons could be learned from something like that?"

"Abandonment comes to mind. Got a lot of those issues."

"What lessons could be learned from abandonment?" he asks.

As she thinks about it, she looks down at the shiny blade and her reflection staring back. What she sees is an inquisitiveness in her eyes. It's obvious she's never thought about this before.

"Abandonment. I don't know. I'm more reliant on myself and not on others. Which makes me more of a loner. But why would I chose something like that in the first place?"

"Life is a school. Who knows why we choose the courses we do? Anyway, there're a lot of theories out there. It might do you some good to look into them. But hypothetical or not, owning our situations helps us more than feeling victimized by them."

Winster drops back in his seat. That's all he's going to say about it. The rest is up to her. Her eyes shift from him as she filters through the information. For her, it's a new way of thinking about things. A different way. If she did agree to her "pre-life circumstances" for whatever reasons, then there is no one to blame. Not even herself. Blame is for victims. And Stef is no victim. She's a survivor. And survivors are learners. They have to be, in order to survive. So maybe she should be thinking about that and what lessons could be learned about being a survivor? The mere thought of that offers a more positive result than her old way of thinking. This could work for her.

"Is that my stick?" he asks, eager to get his hands on it.

"It's not a stick! It's a *hiking*-stick. There's a difference. It has purpose. Like the knives you're giving me. You refuse to use that cane of yours, so I thought maybe you'd use a hiking stick instead. Especially if I made it."

He inspects the work. It's spiraled like a corkscrew due to the bittersweet vine wrapped around it. The bark is shaved and the wood sanded to a shine. She left a single branch, which serves as a hand-guard in the middle. The stick is four feet long and will have to be shortened to serve as a cane.

"You did this? I'm impressed."

She gestures "yes," and guides him to his feet. She places the hiking stick near his side and takes the smaller of her two knives.

"What are you doing now?"

"Measuring where I need to cut it," she comments.

"Don't forget to leave a few inches for the curved handle,"

he adds.

"How am I going to curve the handle?"

"Boil water in a kettle and hold the stick over the escaping steam. That softens the wood so you can bend it."

"Oh!" She says, surprised at the simplicity of the technique.

Moments later, the kettle whistles as Mr. Winster guides Stef through the steps. She props open the whistler cap to the kettle, allowing a thick flow of steam to escape.

"Now take it and run the area you want to bend over the steam," he says.

Stef bends over, carefully guiding the end of the stick over the escaping steam. Her mom's Egyptian cross-ankh swings into view between her cleavage within the low, buttoned shirt. It catches his eye. It's a good view. What cleavage isn't?

"I do remember reading this somewhere," she says. "I just never got around to trying it." She looks up, catching him looking down her shirt.

"Tell ya what," she says. "Why don't *you* heat the wood and I'll look down *your* shirt?"

"I don't know. I'm pretty sure you'll be getting the short end of the stick on that one."

A short time later, Mr. Winster runs the hiking stick over the escaping steam. She stands by, arms crossed over her chest, considering the eighty-something-year-old man. As she watches him perform his magic on the stick, she finds herself reliving a childhood experience.

She's five years old and in bed. It's dark, but she's not asleep. Her eyes rove over the fluorescent stars on her ceiling. Most of the constellations have been carefully matched to the night sky. There's Orion, the Big Dipper, the Little Dipper, and the Pleiades, along with all of the planets—including Pluto.

The bedroom door opens slowly and light creeps in, washing away her ceiling view. She peeks through closed eyelids at the adult male entering her room. He crosses to her bedside and sits beside her. He lowers the blanket to her waist and unbuttons the bottom couple of buttons to her pajama top. He stops midway, revealing only her stomach. She opens her eyes, seeing the man. He's a handsome man, thirties, wearing a blue t-shirt.

He has facial stubbles from a long day without shaving. His hair is light brown, short and unkept. He's looking at her stomach as a shadow darkens the room. A woman enters, asking, "What are you doing?"

Stef flinches from something poking at her stomach . . .

It's Mr. Winster, and he's poking her with the stick, "Hey, where are you?"

She doesn't know. She's digesting what just happened, trying to hang on to every detail, every moment. Were those her parents? Was that her bedroom? She looks as if she's seen a ghost.

"What's the matter?"

"Would you excuse me for a minute? I have to call Lillian." She races out of the kitchen.

Stef paces back and forth by her truck, phone to her ear. "It had to be my father. Who else could it have been?"

"I don't know," Lillian says through the phone. "Maybe a babysitter . . . and you're sure that was a woman's voice?"

"Absolutely, Lil. What are you thinking? You don't think it was my father?"

"Do you want to think that was your father?"

"No! I mean, I do, but I don't want to think he was . . ."

"Then don't. There's not enough information. Right now we don't know what he was doing with you. But we'll figure that out. Okay? You're probably going to start having more of these, so start documenting them. Keep a journal. Okay? You alright?"

"I'm fine. It just caught me off guard. Thanks, Lillian."

"Night, night."

Stef disconnects her call with Lillian. She's relaxed and grateful she called her. She notices the three quarter moon, then Mr. Winster sitting on the porch with the hiking stick. The handle is curved nicely. She takes a seat next to him, enjoying the night air. They sit in silence, happy for the other's presence.

Stef sits on the couch, cross-legged and relaxed as Lillian crosses from her desk with a cassette and inserts it into her tape player on a table next to her chair.

"Nice shirt," Lillian says. "What'd you do, sleep in it?"

"You can tell?"

"Girl, you have got to be better on behalf of yourself. Now, what are we doing?"

"I want to go back to the truck first," Stef says. "I need to know what happened there."

"Okay, but first I want to know why. And I want the truth."

Stef fidgets in her seat. "Okay—once a month, I go through a major change . . ."

"All women do," Lillian says.

"No! This isn't something that can be fixed with a tampon. We're talking fur, claws, and ass!" She says, with emphasis on the "ass."

"You turn into a werewolf?" Lillian asks sarcastically, almost prepared for the stunning disclosure. Stef doesn't answer. She doesn't have to. Her look says it all. Lillian pushes for more information. "Okay. So, you're a werewolf. What do you want to know? And why?"

Stef is suspicious over Lillian's sudden acceptance. It's obvious she doesn't believe her. But she'll have to go along with it. "That's why I want to know—because I'm a werewolf. What I need to know is who infected me."

"Who infected you!? You mean, turned you into a werewolf!? Who cares who infected you? If you're a werewolf, don't you have bigger problems?"

It's clear to Stef that Lillian's just playing this out. She knows Lillian's good at what she does and that's all she wants. She doesn't need therapy. She needs to be hypnotized.

"The one that infected me has probably infected others. It'd be nice to know who they are so we could talk. Learn from each other."

"Talk. You mean like start a chat-up? What do you want to talk about? Maybe I could help. I did a little reading on werewolves over the weekend."

Stef smiles, knowing she's being patronized. She also knows Lillian doesn't mean anything by it, but Stef will have to stand firm and defend herself. She crosses to Lillian's desk, grabbing a jar filled with trail mix, and returns to the couch.

"Oh, good," Stef says sarcastically. "I feel so much better knowing you did a little reading over the weekend. I want to know if I'll be able to have kids."

"Kids?" Lillian asks surprised. This takes her aback. "Wow! I didn't expect that. Okay. That's a good start. Why do you think you wouldn't be able to have kids?"

"Because I'm a werewolf," Stef says casually, dipping into the jar.

"I don't see how that could be a problem. I mean, why wouldn't a werewolf be able to have children? I didn't read anything about it affecting reproductive organs. I think you'll be fine."

"Oh, thank God. I'm so relieved. Twenty-five years of worrying and all I had to do was ask you. Who knew? Now I'll just have to figure out how to prevent them from eating the neighbors. Just in case they turn out to be carnivorous."

Lillian reclines in her chair, unsure if Stef is serious or not. "Are you being sarcastic with me?"

"No! Why would you think that? You did a little reading over the weekend. Are you kidding me, Lillian? Do you have any idea how serious this is? I don't expect you to believe me, but you don't have to be so goddamn condescending. Be a little open-minded . . ."

"Open-minded? Are you shittin' me? You don't know how lucky you are I'm not strapping your ass in a goddamn straightjacket. I'd say that is pretty friggin' open-minded."

"Straightjacket!?"

"Do you know how batshit crazy you sound right now? I mean, you're a friggin' vegetarian, for Christ's sake. What do you do, raid gardens? I said I wanted the truth. Jesus Christ. You think I'm some kind of idiot?"

"Relax, Lillian. Calm down!"

"You calm down. Pissin' me off, Stefanie. Now, you tell me the truth or you can get the hell out of my office."

"I'm telling the truth. Where am I going this weekend?"

"What? To Maine. What does that have to do with anything?"

"How often do I go?" Stef asks.

"Every month. You're changing the subject."

"What happens while I'm gone, Lillian? In the sky—what happens in the sky?"

Lillian's losing her focus. And control. Now she's the one being put under the microscope. She doesn't know what happens in the sky. She doesn't know anything at this moment. She's starting to cave. "How do I know what happens in the sky? It's light, then dark. What do I look like, a meteorologist?"

Stef gestures for her to check her calendar. Lillian snatches the trail mix out of Stef's hand and takes a bunch. She then marches to her calendar on the wall, not at all happy about it. She navigates past the many hand-scribbled notes, times, and appointments. "Alright, what am I looking for?" she murmurs, looking at the month at a glance. "Monthly events . . ."

After a moment, she notices a consistency. She flips to the previous month, using her finger as a pointer. Then the next. And the next. She repeats this for every month preceding. She then turns back to Stef. "Big deal!"

"Didn't you find it curious I was always unavailable on full moon nights?"

"To be honest, I never noticed."

"Come on, Lillian. Even Mr. Winster noticed."

"You told him you're a werewolf?"

"No! I didn't tell him. But he noticed I go to Maine every month. Which is more than I can say for you."

"I'm a therapist—not a goddamn astronomer."

"You're outside, bored, and lonely, 'cause your best friend isn't around every friggin' full moon night. I mean, Jesus, pay a little attention already."

"Shove it, Stefanie! Got to be a goddam detective just to be your friend. It's not like I forgot your birthday . . ."

She did forget her birthday, evidenced by the blank stare Stef is wearing.

"You're gonna bring that up again?" Lillian asks. "I forgot one time."

"How many times have I forgotten your birthday?"

"Never let me live that down."

"You know how many? None! You know how I know? 'Cause I remember things I forget. Sometimes! But you don't even remember forgetting. I don't know what's worse. You forgetting my birthday or forgetting you forgot."

"Okay! Okay! Okay! I'm a bad friend. Maybe I should have just told you I was busy shoving lightning up Frankenstein's ass for a date-night."

"Shows how much you know. Frankenstein was the scientist, not the monster." Stef realizes this is going nowhere fast and starts searching for her bag, announcing, "If you're gonna be an ass, be an accurate one."

"Is that like, 'If you're going to spread the bullshit, spread it thick . . . ?' "

Stef isn't responding to her. Lillian snatches her bag before Stefanie sees it and holds it up, baiting her. "Looking for this?"

Stef reaches for it, but Lillian keeps it from her. Stef's not in the mood for making up right now.

"You know what? Keep the damn thing." Stef marches for the door, leaving Lillian on the other side of the room.

Lillian announces with authority, "Sit your ass down! Now!"

Stef turns in defiance, crossing her arms, waiting on her bag.

"You made me promise not to tell anyone," Lillian says. "You didn't say anything about making fun of you. Now stop acting like a child and sit down. You have to know there's no way I can believe you actually turn into a werewolf. I mean, did you even think about that just a little?"

"I didn't have to think about it. I told you so I could get hypnotized. You're the one who wanted to know why."

Stef marches back to the couch and drops into a seated position, demanding, "Now apologize!"

"Screw you. I'm not apologizing. Kiss my ass," Lillian says, defiantly. In fact, you owe me an apology for wasting my time. There's no way in hell I'm going to believe you're a werewolf. And by the way you're acting, if you were raped, you're hiding something you don't want me to know. And that's flat-out wasting my time. But you know what? I'm going to hypnotize you regardless. Because that's the kind of friend I am. And you don't even have to apologize."

"I'm not hiding anything from you, Lillian. And I apologize if you think I am."

Lillian can't understand her. She knows Stef has to be hiding something and the only way she's going to get to the bottom of it is to get on with the session. But in order for her to begin, Stef has to be relaxed. And she isn't. She's tense and withdrawn. Obviously, there's a lot riding on this for Stef.

Lillian pours two shots of brandy and hands one to Stef, studying her shirt. "Where'd you get that shirt, Good Will?" Lillian asks. "Steal it from someone's locker? I ask, because I know it's something you'd never buy. It's too expensive. Or at least it was."

"It was on sale," Stef announces proudly, ignoring her insults, with, "At least, that's what I was told."

"Who told you that?" Lillian asks doubtfully.

Stef is looking at her. Oh, boy. Lillian forgot she gave it to her.

"You probably snatched it out of your rag bag as a last-minute gift 'cause you forgot it was my birthday. Didn't you?"

Lillian sips her brandy, avoiding eye contact.

"Oh, my God, you did!" Stef says, somewhat shocked, but not really.

Lillian starts laughing. "It wasn't a rag then. It was going to be."

"That's comforting," Stef says, not really surprised.

"You're very easy to shop for," Lillian blurts out, laughing, this time at her own joke.

"Yeah!" Stef announces. "It's Stef's birthday, let's see what I can dig up out of the trash for her."

"It's your own fault, you know. If you cared about what you wore, I'd care more about what I gave you."

"I'd stop now while I was ahead," Stef warns.

"Oh, good. And I thought you were upset with me. You know, you're not an easy person to be friends with."

Stef isn't saying a word, nor is she reacting to the ongoing attacks. She's just taking it all in, waiting.

Lillian notices, offering, "God in Heaven, I'm sorry.

You're very easy to be friends with. It's being your friend that's difficult. You set a very high bar for friendship."

"What high bar? You're my best friend. Therefore, I think of you more than I think of myself."

"Oh, that's just hurtful, Stefanie. Very, very hurtful."

"Well . . . I'm sorry."

"And for the record," Lillian adds, "I'm more than your best friend. I'm all the family you have. That's a lot of shit to cover."

"It is, isn't it?" Stef says.

"Right? A lot of shit. I've carried your ass from one drama to the next, one apartment to the next, and now this. Lay your ass down and let's get on with it. Take on some more of your shit. More role-playing than a Hollywood extra."

Stef bursts out laughing. Lillian loves it when Stef laughs at her jokes. Lillian takes a fresh cassette tape and unwraps the plastic cover.

"That's pretty good. I like that."

"Thank you. I just made that up. Okay, time to relax," Lillian says, adding, "I hope Rin Tin Tin bites you in the ass this time."

"Thanks. His name is Ominous, by the way. I mean, that's how I refer to him."

"Ominous? I like that. If he doesn't like the name, I'd love to have it. I'll name my next kitty after him."

"Come on, Lillian. He has a name. I just don't know what it is. That's why I'm here. So put me under, keep me under, and you can have the damn name. Focus! I need you with me on this. It's going to get scary, but I survive."

"Oh, thank God," Lillian replies, more focused on unwrapping the plastic from the cassette tape.

Stef sits up, shooting a look of frustration at her.

"Now what?" asks, Lillian.

"Where are you?"

"I'm here."

"You're not here. It's like you got a cake in the oven, for Christ's sake."

"I'm here. Lie back and shut up. Here we go. Relax. I'll play a little background music to ease your mind."

Hard rock booms from the speakers—"Sorry about that. How's your other ear?"

Stef queries, "People actually pay for these sessions?"

"Amazing, isn't it?" Lillian jokes. "I'd have walked out by now. Alright, down you go, and you are relaxed. From your toes to your ankles . . . to your knees and your thighs, leave your body behind as you get hyp-no-tized."

"Can you just put me under without the goddamn poetry? Jesus Christ, I feel like I'm in a session with Snoop Dog."

"That wasn't Snoop Dog. That was mine. I'm sorry. I thought I'd throw it out there."

"Well, throw it someplace else . . ."

"There's no room. You got the market cornered with this werewolf bullshit."

Stef rolls off of the couch, laughing, taking Lillian with her. The two swat at each other, rolling across the floor, laughing.

Finally, there's silence in the room. A breeze blows the curtain out from the window as . . .

"I smell wet fur . . ."

"I smell wet fur . . ."

The image is as clear as when ten-year-old Steffy left it. Ominous, the dark, menacing creature, claws at the window of the truck, trying to get in. He's so close she can smell him. That's what it is! He was most likely in the fields when the sprinklers went off. She cowers deeper into the shadows, but she can still see his pupils focusing in on her.

He's fearsome, yet mindless, without conscience or caution. He's curious. Very, very curious. Her only protection is the thin glass barrier between them and it's open about an inch.

She has to do something. There's no one else around. There has to be a way out of this.

His claws land on the opened window edge and he freezes, looking at it. He's just found a way in. But now what? He works his claws inside and slowly pulls on the glass. This is a new discovery for him.

For her, time is running out. She edges closer to the driver's side and out of reach just as he breaks the glass halfway down. He rips it out, then works on the bottom half.

She scrambles up to the driver's door, absolutely terrified. He stops and watches her.

Where is she going? What is she doing? He studies the glass, running his claws over it. He cuts himself. Blood drips from his hands. He won't make that mistake again. He grabs the glass and yanks it out of the door frame. He reaches into the truck, trying to grab her. She's coiled up tight against the door, pulling on the handle, but it's stuck. She bounces her shoulder off of the door, trying to force it open, but it's not working.

He reaches across the seat for her. She slaps at him. He tries for her ankles, ripping the seat to shreds with his long claws.

Suddenly, a distraction. Something alerts him from the field. He can smell it. He leans into the door, vying for cover, waiting. It approaches fast.

Stefanie has had it. She's mad and getting madder. He looks at her and she at him. She lunges at him from across the seat, yelling, "Get away from me. Get away! I lost my necklace because of you, now get away."

Ominous is stunned by this. He watches her intently, startled by her yelling and screaming. Suddenly, he viciously attacks the glass. Then the door. He's beating and punching the metal frame. Stef is slapping the seat, ready to go head to head with him. She's clearly had enough of this bullying.

Suddenly, the driver's door is pulled open from the outside as a furry paw grabs Stef by the shoulder and yanks her from the vehicle. She's thrown several yards away in the grass. As she looks up, she sees a second werewolf turning back to the truck, ready to face Ominous. He's a smaller werewolf. A familiar werewolf. A mini-wolf.

Ominous looks across the driver's seat at him. Instead of racing around the truck, he tears the glass from the door and claws his way viciously towards mini-wolf. Ominous reaches the driver's side, placing his hands on the door jamb. Mini-wolf, waiting patiently for this, slams the door closed on Ominous' paws, trapping him in the truck. He howls in pain.

Mini-wolf then turns to Stef, who's watching in horror from the ground. He moves slowly towards her, but she's not going to have any of that with him, either. She lunges for him. But mini-wolf controls her arms and tries settling her down.

She stops fighting and withdraws her attack. He extends his fur-covered paw, revealing her necklace.

"Ralf," she murmurs, looking at his ripped clothing. "Is that you?"

He growls "yes," possibly unable to speak.

"Get me out of here. Now!"

Ralf lifts her up with ease and carries her out of the area and into the woods. Ralf, aka mini-wolf, lays Stef against a tree. She's safe. She touches his fur, then studies his pointy ears and dark, leathery nose. How could this be?

"What happened to you?" she asks.

He rises, suspicious of something. Just then, like a streak of lightning, Ominous blasts through the forest, tackling him. The fight is on. Mini-wolf, although smaller, is just as strong as Ominous and holds his own against him. It's a brutal fight. Their clothes are shredded. Pieces of fur light above the ground, reflected by the moonlight. Soil and shrubs are kicked loose as the two lay into each other.

Ominous gets a grip on mini-wolf and throws him towards Stef. He bounces off the tree and falls limply to the ground next to her. Stef pulls him over, protecting him.

Ominous is curious over this. What does she want with him? And why? But then he catches a scent of her. It's irresistible. He can't ignore it and draws close.

Ominous reaches out with his sharp, black claws and slides her sleeve up. Stef is too confused to fight back. She relents, waiting for the inevitable. Ominous moves to her pant leg and slides it above her calf. Whatever he's looking for isn't there. Next, he goes for her shirt, pulling it up to inspect her stomach. He's looking for something, but what?

Mini-wolf opens his eyes, noticing Ominous. He grabs

Ominous's claws. They struggle. Stef tucks her knees away from the flailing claws, but it's too late. There's a slash. Both mini-wolf and Ominous look at Stef's stomach. Her shirt is ripped open and she's bleeding. It's not a fatal wound, but it is a permanent one. One that will change her life forever. Mini-wolf regards the shirt material sticking to his claws. He did it. He scratched Stef. And all three notice this. Ominous grabs mini-wolf and throws him. He then dives on him, leaving Stef alone. She scrambles to her feet, running off, leaving Ralf and Ominous to their battle.

Later, Lillian stares at Stef, sipping from a brandy glass. "I'm going with you this weekend. I'll need to see this with my own eyes."

"She doesn't play well with others," Stef says, taking a swig from her brandy.

"She . . . as in you? Have you killed anybody?"

"Me? No!"

"Has she killed anybody?"

"You can ask her when you see her."

The two stare at each other. It's clear Stef is trying to scare Lillian off. But Lillian isn't going to budge. She's going. Then, slowly, Stef reveals a smile behind the brandy glass held close to her lips. It could be she's beginning to like the idea of Lillian going, seeing, knowing about her. It could be a good thing.

It could be.

You Get What You Pay For

Dave D'Alessio

THE CELL PHONE FOOTAGE WAS shaky, but Tanaba could see the subject well enough. It was a green monster covered with scales that glittered in the sunlight as it rumbled through Oslo's residential suburb. Taller than the three-story buildings, a line of plates ran down its spine, orienting toward the sun as it waded forward inexorably, its heavy tail battering houses apart as terrified Norwegians ran for their lives.

"Turn the sound on, please." Tanaba was the President of Terra; these were his people suffering.

Shouts and screams filled the conference room. Tanaba knew no Norwegian, but he knew the sound of fear in any language. He and his cabinet bore the responsibility of governing Earth, and now also protecting it. They watched the recordings from the Presidential Palace in Geneva, safe for the moment, but still horrified.

The monster turned to face the camera and opened its mouth. The sound it made was unearthly, more metallic screech than animal roar. It breathed deeply and belched a lightning bolt that lit the city with white light. The bolt grounded through a streetlight, heating it and glowing red hot before it melted to slag.

The image broke up. "He dropped the phone and ran," Tanaba's aide, Yates, said.

"Wise man." Tanaba pushed his spectacles up his nose. "What else happened?"

Yates didn't consult his notes. "It went to the Scatec Solar plant and connected directly into their circuits somehow. Scatec says power levels dropped ninety-five percent in the next three minutes."

Yates whispered, "Almost ten thousand homes flooded." Like most coastal cities, Oslo was protected by sea walls since the ice caps melted; the beast simply kicked holes through them when it emerged.

"And then it waded back into the fjord," Tanaba said. "Just walked away until it was underwater."

Defense Minister Johnson's face was even redder than usual. "If we had a navy worth discussing, we could track that damned thing. If we had a proper army, we could fight it. But no! Damned socialism, always buying entitlements with our tax dollars . . ."

Tanaba said, "Thank you, Minister Johnson," and pushed his spectacles up again. Tanaba was from the lost nation of Kiribati, her islands submerged during the twenty-first century global warming. Kiribati had never had an army or a navy; perhaps what worked for her was insufficient for an entire planet. "I understand the chaps at Google are tracking it by satellite. The question is, 'What shall we do now?' Minister Yuan?"

Across the table, Science Minister Yuan wore his usual bland expression. "It is clearly not of terrestrial origin."

The Melanesian equivalent of "Clearly" was redundant, and so Tanaba did not say it. Instead, he said, "Perhaps I should contact the United Planets ambassador for advice." Tanaba met Ambassador Mrwip, a meter-tall decapod, at his inauguration.

His cabinet did not approve. "Outrageous." "Nonsense. This is our problem to solve." "Are we children, running to Mommy at the first sign of danger?" "Can't let those commie aliens know we're weak." "The loss of face for our planet would be intolerable."

Tanaba was President of Earth because no member nation of the Terra Unity Party objected when his name was put forward; no one objected to him because he rarely objected to anyone else. "Then I shall not," he said. He pushed his spectacles up again—the rigors of office left him no time for corrective surgery—and thought, *I shall not yet.*

Google's engineers tracked the monster as it moved with surprising rapidity underwater; the scant visual imagery suggested its enormous tail propelled it, much like a dolphin or a whale. Its path pointed like an arrow across the North Sea to Scotland. Estimated landfall: three days.

Tanaba warned the Queen, who ordered an evacuation of the coast.

When the creature emerged from the waters off Dunfermline, the Scots Guards were waiting behind the line of dikes that kept the rising seas away from the town. Tanaba and his cabinet watched via live feed as the Guards dug into the hills and threw up sand-bagged strongpoints around the evacuated village. Six antique tanks, exhumed from the dustbin of history, trundled forward to do battle.

The monster brushed the brave soldiers aside with sweeps of its tail, picked up a tank and hurled it into the sea. Artillery rounds provoked lightning breath responses, and the monster slapped anti-tank rockets away as though they were mosquitos. It waddled to an industrial park and hunkered down, its roars sounding almost ecstatic.

"That's the babyHydro plant," Yates murmured. "Reports are that power is draining from the Scottish grid at record levels. Edinburgh is already blacked out." On the screen, the monster lay down, as though to nap.

Tanaba wondered whether it was his imagination, or was the creature growing as they watched? He pushed his spectacles up for a better view. It certainly seemed larger than it had mere minutes before.

If it was growing, the monster's destructive power could only increase as it got larger. He said, "If no one has any better ideas, I'm going to contact the United Planets."

"Nonsense!" "Outrageous!" "I shall be forced to resign if you pursue a course so antithetical to the future of this planet!" "And I!" "Me, too!"

"Then perhaps someone would like to make a suggestion?" Tanaba said.

Johnson seemed unusually smug. "I think we can show you a little something, Mr. President."

"If you would be so kind."

Two days later, now twenty-five meters tall, the monster swam down the English Channel. The north coast of France held its breath. Minister Johnson murmured into his phone, directing TV drones to keep pace with the swimming beast as it cruised past the Cotentin peninsula and turned south. "It seems to be attracted to renewable power sources," Minister Yuan said blandly. "It has ignored several French nuclear plants."

Tanaba said, "Then where would you guess it is headed?" He polished his spectacles on the end of his tie.

Yuan called a map up on their display screen. "There is a tidal power plant here, near Dinan. If it intends to head there, it will enter the estuary at Saint-Malo."

"Hah! I've got you now, you bastard!" Johnson no longer kept his voice down as he shouted orders into his phone. "I'll be ready for you this time!"

Tanaba used his authority to order Saint-Malo evacuated, at great expense, and the inhabitants compensated, at greater expense. The evacuations would prevent the loss of life, but the destruction of property . . . if the monster punched a hole in her levees, all of Saint-Malo would flood just as Kiribati had. The damages? Already over a billion sols and rising as the disruptions to lives and the world power grid savaged the economy.

The old city of Dinan was bombed to rubble two centuries before during World War II, and now stood as a monument to mid-twentieth century construction, with graceful forms of arching concrete and glittering glass walls that shattered brilliantly into snows of shards under the monster's feet. It waded through the empty city, its roars and the screeching of police whistles breaking the silence. Its roars, the screeching of police whistles . . . and the whine of a supersonic unmanned aircraft.

"I thought they had all been recycled," Tanaba said. A dividend of peace and planetary unity: no one needed combat drones any longer. Now the nations of the world fought together against rising seas, rather than against each other.

Johnson watched the video screen, a grin of triumph across his face. "Got it out of the Udvar-Hazy museum in Virginia. It was hanging there, just in case we needed it someday."

"Disgraceful," Dikembe said, and Chakrobarty, the Minister of Economics, added, "Wasteful." Muttered sentiment ran against Johnson.

As for himself, Tanaba suspected that America was not the only member nation with something 'hanging there, just in case.' "Now is not the time, ladies and gentlemen," he said. If they still had a planet left when the monster was done, then they could worry about who was breaking which treaties

Tanaba watched as the beast hunkered down in the wreckage of an electrical substation, draining energy from France's power lines. It seemed to be growing again, growing in height, growing in bulk, growing in might. "How could such a thing have grown?" he whispered. "Is this only a baby?"

Yuan must have heard. "There is conjecture that it spawned and matured near an undersea hydrothermal vent. That would provide a convenient source of energy."

"Figure it out later, during the autopsy," Johnson said. "Just watch this."

Tanaba pushed his spectacles into place.

On the screen the drone dove toward the beast. The monster looked directly at it, opened its mouth to unleash its furies on the whining intruder.

The drone dropped a single bomb, laser-guided directly to its target. The bomb flew straight down the monster's throat.

Tanaba sighed in relief.

The bomb detonated.

The beast belched a plume of smoke, and then obliterated the drone with a lightning discharge, the flash blinding their local camera. In the future, the children of Virginia would have to go to a different museum to learn about historic aircraft.

"I shall consult the United Planets ambassador," Tanaba said. "Yates, would you be so good as to get her on the phone?"

"Nonsense!" "Outrageous!" "I shall be forced to resign if you pursue a course so antithetical to the future of this planet!" "And I!" "Me, too!"

"Ladies and gentlemen, if this government collapses in the middle of a crisis because of your unreasoned xenophobia, we will lose any opportunity to take any action at all." Tanaba had prepared this speech beforehand, hoping not to need it. But the beast was still unharmed and reports were already trickling in of damage to the European power grid: trains stopped, lights out, hospitals on emergency generators. "And if we choose that path, then is it likely that we will fall along with the government. How long before mob rule? Before martial law? Before we return to the jungle?" He looked around the room at all their faces, set and grim. "I will take full responsibility, of course."

"Bet yer ass," Johnson said.

Ambassador Mrwip was from a planet with a chlorine atmosphere, so Tanaba was unable to meet her—at this point in Mrwip's life cycle she was a her, and would continue to be for another Terran year or so—face to face. On Scype, most of Mrwip's legs were hidden, and her fur reminded Tanaba of a cat's, so her only truly disconcerting features were her third and fourth eyes.

"I dislike to disturb you, but we are in a crisis and I was hoping to ask your advice," Tanaba said. He tried to focus his attention on the two of Mrwip's eyes that Yuan's scientists assured him operated in the visual spectrum. "You must have seen what has transpired."

Between Mrwip's fur and her alien nature, it was hard to read her face. "Yes." She spoke Terran English with a thick accent. "We have had a loss of power here at the Embassy as well. Would you like me to contact someone? A specialist, perhaps?"

"If you would be so kind," Tanaba said. It was not until after they exchanged further pleasantries and signed off that it occurred to him: a specialist in whatever that thing was? Could they be so common in the universe that people specialized in them?

The United Planets were known to have faster-than-light technology; it would be impossible for United Planets to exist without it. How much faster than light was still unknown to Terran scientists, although they got a great deal of useful data when a new ship appeared in Earth orbit just one week later. It was large and boxy—typical, Yuan assured Tanaba, of a freighter or other innocuous craft. It slipped into a geocentric orbit 36,000 kilometers above Ghana.

Humanity had already met four alien races and knew of twenty more, but the entity on the screen in front of Tanaba was from none of the familiar peoples. Its face was bilaterally symmetrical, for which Tanaba was grateful, and it had two eyes and a single mouth. It also had iridescent orange scales running down its face and a tuft of reddish feathers standing straight up from its head. "Greetings, leader of Terra people," it said via Google Translate. "I am leader Gggawk. We Sertian people. Mrwip call we. You having pest problem, yes-no?"

Pest? The monster had just left Bilbao a smoking ruin; the natural gas generator had overloaded from the strain of the monster's feeding, and exploded. Yates had said damages were climbing toward fifty billions; Chakrobarty's projections showed the global economy zooming past recession and heading toward depression without passing Go or collecting twenty sols. "Yes," Tanaba said.

Gggawk squawked, "Is common problem. Comes from bad washing of ships. Probably lousy Ongkliks. You have Ongklik ship visit, yes-no?"

An Ongklik diplomatic spacecraft had been among the first to visit Earth, before Tanaba was President. Their visit dominated the news as far away as Fiji, where Tanaba was a local mayor at the time. "Yes, we did," he said. "How do people solve . . . um . . . problems like this?"

"How I solve, my business," Gggawk said. "How you solve, easy. Give we one trillion sols. Gold good. Diamonds, too. We make it go away."

Chakrobarty shook her head frantically. "Global depression," she stage-whispered.

156

"How large will it grow?" Tanaba said, pushing his spectacles up. He needed time, and he needed information.

"It keep eating, it keep growing." Gggawk said. "Bigger it get, bigger my fee."

Tanaba muted the conversation and turned to his cabinet for advice. "Shall I accept?"

"Nonsense!" "Outrageous!" "I shall be forced to resign if you pursue a course so antithetical to the future of this planet!" "And I!" "Me, too!"

But what else was there to do? Tanaba used his personal phone to contact Mrwip and fill her in. "Is that a fair price?"

The felinoid groomed with her uppermost two paws. "I believe a common statement on your planet is, 'You get what you pay for,' Mister President."

One trillion sols. One hundred sols each from every man, woman, and child on the planet. A billion of them barely made that much in a year: subsistence farmers, refugees from rising tides, people fleeing desertification on four continents.

Tanaba peered at the screen. Google placed the monster off the coast of Portugal, swimming south. Tuan expected the Gibraltar tidal barrage to be its next stop. The barrage supplied power to southwest Europe and northwest Africa, to four million households plus hospitals, businesses, and mass transit. Its electricity ran the pumps keeping the historic cities of Rome and Tangiers from joining poor, drowned Venice under water.

"We accept," he said, over the howls of his cabinet.

Having agreed to the Sertian terms, Tanaba announced tax increases and suppressed protests before they turned violent. He had the planet's gold supplies trucked out of vaults in London, Frankfort, Beijing, and a half dozen other cities, including, over Minister Johnson's vigorous protests, Fort Knox. The English Crown Jewels, the Kohinoor diamond, the Star Sapphire of India . . . all requisitioned, "paid" for with inflationary paper sols well on their way to valuelessness. Tanaba had the goods, exactly one trillion sols worth, placed in containers sent to the surface by the Sertian spacecraft. The containers returned to orbit.

When the monster, now forty meters tall, waded ashore just inside the Pillars of Hercules, the vast Sertian cargo ship, a hundred times more voluminous than the largest spacecraft ever launched by Earth, descended to wait for it. It hovered just above the Mediterranean on a propulsion system so alien even Minister Tuan's eyebrows raised two millimeters. Two hatch doors swung open to the sides, and from behind them, tiny winged rockets streaked forth. The little ships buzzed around the beast's head, deftly avoiding lightning breaths, snapping teeth, and hurled detritus. On the screen Tanaba could see them using some form of beam weapon, strong enough to irritate, not powerful enough to injure.

The creature howled and swatted at the tiny ships, its tail thrashing the warm Mediterranean waters to foam. It took one step forward, then another, all the while screeching with rage. The little flyers deftly herded it toward the large ship, their beams singeing it from all sides but one.

Seeking refuge from the mites harassing it, the beast sought refuge behind the ship's hatchway doors, ducking its head step inside. The great doors swung closed behind it, and the ship elevated, propelled back into orbit by some means no Earthly instruments could measure.

A trillion sols squeezed out of the planetary economy beggared the planet. Over the next few weeks, one hundred sol banknotes, the few still in circulation, were useful only as coffee filters; the far more common ones and tens were stamped with an extra three zeroes to make them viable. Unemployment soared past twenty-five percent and still ascended, crime waves swept the planet from Kalamazoo to Timbuktu, and bread lines sprouted in the few cities not wracked by food riots.

Tanaba's government resigned en masse, and Tanaba could see that the next election would have roughly one hundred eighty-three member nations of the Terra Unity Party who would object to his continuing in office. Only Yates remained, although no longer on salary; the government could no longer afford luxuries like aides.

To be frank, Tanaba didn't want to be President. He would take it if he was given a chance to clean up the mess, but that seemed unlikely. Until the election, though, someone had to sit in the office. He polished his spectacles and vowed to have the corrective surgery during the free time he would soon have.

In that time, the Sertian ship departed from the Solar System and returned, presumably freed of its monstrous burden. Leader Gggawk contacted Tanaba from orbit, although Tanaba could not imagine why.

"Yes, Leader," he said. "Is there something else I can do for you?"

Gggawk said, "New zoo on Metabelis wanted that bad boy bad. Wanted say thanks."

If Earth had developed interstellar flight on its own, she could have shared in that. But alas. And for years in the future there would be paltry few funds for Research and Development, not when there were people to feed. "Well, then, congratulations," Tanaba said. "And you have our gratitude to removing that . . . that thing before it destroyed the entire planet."

Gggawk seemed little interested in Terra's gratitude. It groomed its tuft feathers with a talon and flicked away something too small for Tanaba to see. "You, Terra leader," he said. "You okay for new boy. Say what, next time we do two for same price, yes-no?"

"Two? One nearly destroyed the planet! How could two survive together?" Tanaba said. A creature that destroyed its own environment? How could there even be one of such a thing, let alone two?

Gggawk preened before answering. "Terra leader. Many things possible. Big universe out there!"

The Chorus from the Hive

Edward Ahern

"HAVE YOU EVER NOTICED THAT man never dreamed up any insect gods?"

"Only an entomologist would think of that, Leslie."

"Look at those carpenter ants. To comprehend an insect god, Robbie, we'd probably have to have a hive mind."

Robbie put down his gin and tonic and stared at her. Her eyes hadn't shifted from the ants marching in a loose line across their deck. "I'm sure you're wrong, Les. The Egyptians had beetles."

Leslie's mouth puckered and she shook her head, the blue dyed patch of hair swinging loose. Robbie was lovable but sometimes pedestrian. "The Egyptians had scarabs. They were personified by a humanistic god called Khepni. And the

Greeks had a wimp god called Tithonus who was in charge of cicadas, of all things. And that's it."

Robbie shrugged. He didn't give a damn about bug theology, but knew when Leslie was winding up into one of her compulsions. "Maybe we just can't bond with an exoskeleton deity."

"I'm deadly serious." She shifted her eyes to Robbie, her expression set. "Maybe the insects believe in something we can't conceive of unless we enter their consciousness."

"And maybe we're not capable of doing that."

"Stay with me here. Merely studying insect behavior without understanding their group mentality is only partial knowledge." Leslie pulled back inside herself, her eyes shuttered and unseeing. She said nothing for ten minutes until, "I'll be getting most of the summer off. I need you to cover for me, Robbie—to make excuses for me while I do this."

Robbie frowned. "Do what?"

"Live with the insects. Install a mini house at their colony. Keep my mind open and unfocused until something registers."

Robbie hopped up from his recliner and leaned over her. "That's insane, sweetie. Disease, insect bites, infections . . ." He took her hand. "People like you study bugs, they don't take them into bed with them. Set up cameras, like everybody else does."

Leslie jumped up, her head just reaching his shoulder. "There'll be cameras, and I'll do a documentary that PBS might like. But I'll be trying to measure and mesh with the trillions of entities that we ignore."

She had that look that meant further argument was hopeless. "Ah, Les, at least do it here on our property, so I can watch out for you."

"We may not have enough bugs."

"We might. The rotted oaks back in the woods are loaded with beetles and termites. There's bees and wasps near the old pasture, and ants pretty well everywhere. You can set up platforms and shoot video down into their nests."

Leslie allowed herself a victory smile. "I know you care. And termites are a strong possibility. But forget the platforms, I'll be digging a habitat hole and living with the termites—if you're okay with a trench in our woods."

"It's a terrible idea, Les. Let's go down to Cabo San Lucas instead. Plenty of bugs there."

Her posture stiffened. "I'm doing it. Here or somewhere else, but I'm doing it. Are you going to help me? The foundation would probably pay for almost all of it."

Robbie suspected it would. "I don't care about the hole. I care about you. Hire an expendable technician."

Leslie touched his shoulder. "I love your concern. But the purpose of the experiment is to get beyond the physical and chemical communications—to pry open the insect psyches. Alpha wave measurements, sure, but also try and personally sense collective feeling. We can do it with individual cats and dogs, maybe even dolphins. If I demonstrate arthropodal thought, I'd be set for academic life, not to mention awards, TV appearances and book deals. So. I need to excavate."

"Okay, but I get to shut it down if something goes bad."

Leslie was already a long way down a different thought corridor. "What? Oh. Yeah, sure."

Leslie found a landscaper to handle the excavation, and a retired mechanical engineer who, in turn, found a steel shipping container eight feet long by five feet wide by five feet deep. This he ventilated, electrified, and padded. At Leslie's insistence, he added sliding windows and screens on one side. A metal hatch on the top of the box would let her drop in and scramble out.

Soldier termites swarmed over the backhoe as it gouged out rocks and roots, but minutes later seemed to disappear, and didn't reemerge when a container was dropped into the hole and packed in with rubble and dirt. It was as if the world of men was merely a temporary nuisance.

Five weeks after her idea sprouted, the container was rigged and ready. The night the teeny habitat was powered up, she took Robbie out to dinner.

Once they'd eaten and shared a bottle of wine, she reached across the table and patted his hand. "I'm about to put us through something that will get gnarly. I apologize in advance."

"Les, let me go in there with you. I couldn't do it every day, but I can spend the day with you once or twice a week, and bring supper most days."

She shook her head but smiled. "I need you to be my minder, Robbie, not my companion. The readings and infrared photography are automated, but I need to alter my consciousness. That means occupying the box day and night. I'll be fasting and taking a mix of psychedelic drugs and peyote. I could become incoherent, so you'll need to keep watch. I'll be dirty and testy. I'll understand if you want to hire a real caretaker."

"Not a chance. Nobody's going to watch out for you but me. What about ventilation for this sweat box?"

"Small fans at the vents for air intake and exhaust."

"Jesus, Les, what a miserable summer vacation. You'll probably start growing a fungus."

"Maybe. Let's go home and shed clothes. It'll be our last night together for a while."

The few words they exchanged on the drive home were banal gossip about neighbors and academic misdoings. Neither mentioned the steel box planted among bugs.

Once they got home they made vigorous love, but with the monotonal motions of a spa work-out rather than a romantic tangling. Leslie got up at five a.m. the next morning while Robbie was still sleeping, peed, and went out to start living inside the box. Flush plumbing would be an impossible luxury for the next week.

The coffin—a term she used—was equipped with rations and water, a tiny chemical port-a-pot, lined tablets and pens, and a space blanket. Wired-in electricity powered infrared, externally-mounted cameras, and monitors that measured temperature, sounds, pH, and pheromone levels. A cell phone booster was installed to make sure the signal got through metal and earth. A sound scanner detected ultra-low and ultra-high frequency transmissions. Anything she'd forgotten or ran out of, Robbie could bring her.

Leslie stared at the coffin cuddled against the termite nest. The hatch lid had no latch or locking mechanism—Robbie had insisted she be able to climb out without delay. She dropped down with an inch of space on either hip, pulled the hatch back down, and crouched in dimness. The infrared lighting into the hive showed only a few six-legged, wingless worker termites. Leslie had told Robbie that boredom would be a necessary prelude to any achievement, and her expression was one of suffering patience.

She dosed herself with enough lysergic acid diethylamide and peyote to float slightly above incoherence, and settled in just before the drugs did. Her thoughts wandered off and got lost.

When Leslie drifted back into focus, four hours had passed. She had no memory of visions and felt only confusion. She checked the readings and dials and saw nothing significant. Her back ached from the cramped position she'd been sitting in when she spaced out. She sipped a little water while dropping a half-tab of the acid and resettled herself into a more comfortable position. *Slow and boring, sweetheart, slow and boring.*

As things began to fuzz, she noticed that perhaps a hundred of the quarter-inch termites were perched on the other side of the screen window, as if spectating. *At least I've got an audience.* This time she was out for over five hours, and urgently needed to urinate. She crawled over to the chemical toilet, fumbling with her pants in the cramped space, not quite getting her bottoms off before letting fly. *Memo to self: keep your pants off when you're in here.*

Leslie was also stomach-growlingly hungry and went through an entire prepackaged ration in minutes. As she chewed, she felt vertigo sloshing in and out of her, washing over a headache. It was a possible symptom of progress, and she noted the sensations in her log. She felt her forehead, but didn't have a temperature. Then she glanced at the mesh on the other side of the glass window. Termites were steadily climbing on and off the screen. *Like tourists*, she thought, and laughed at herself.

I need to keep Robbie from panicking. Time to report in. Leslie picked up her cell and called the house.

"Les, Jesus, are you all right?

"Of course, aside from my jeans being a little damp."

"Huh?"

"Never mind. I'm fine." She glanced at her watch, a useless gesture, since she was days away from reemerging.

She could almost see Robbie's expression through the wire. "This is a bad idea. Come home for a while, clean up. I'll feed you."

"Enticing, but that's bad for what I need to do. Busy, busy, Robbie. Got to go. Love you."

She hung up and looked back at the screen. *Termites on, termites off. I wonder.*

Leslie reached over and slid back the glass window, leaving only fine mesh between her and the black crawlers. They seemed unconcerned. She decided to hold off scoring more acid until she'd checked the recorded measurements. There was a deadly lack of activity on all the sensors, and Leslie wondered if she wasn't on an idiot's quest that she could never talk about without facing ridicule.

The second day was as agonizingly boring as the first. She started doodling on the tablet, then stopped when she realized that in a few days she'd run out of paper. The phone call to

Robbie was disjointed. She'd miscalculated her LSD dosage, and Robbie knew she was rezoned for incoherent. The afternoon of the third day, she was wallowing in drugged woe-is-me when one of the instruments flashed. Leslie noted the time, and realized that there was an unseen sunset going on above ground. The low frequency scanner showed an impossibly low hertz level.

Humans can only begin to hear at sixteen hertz. A few animals can hear further down the scale—to perhaps five or six hertz. But the machine had registered vigorous activity at a fraction of one hertz, infrasound usually only noted when an earthquake is setting up.

Well, roast my tits with garlic. What's happening here?

The infrasound modulated for almost a minute longer, then subsided and disappeared. Leslie crawled about checking the other devices, but only the ultra-low sound had occurred, no tremors, no insect activity. Then she noted that the number of termites on her screen had gone from a hundred or so to zero, as if they had other chores.

Could this be bug sing? Some kind of arthropodal barbershop harmony?

Leslie struggled through acid-clouded thought, then set her alarm for ten minutes before sunrise, sucked down her six-hourly quarter tab of LSD, and went to sleep. Her dreams were not of termites, but of ragged winds blowing through episodes of her life.

When the alarm went off, she opened and closed her lips like a fish in air. Her mouth was dry-clotted and nasty, as if she'd been breathing toxins. And maybe she had. The window to the hive was still open and there was an acrid smell wafting in.

Leslie dumped water in her mouth and sloshed it around to clear out the crud. Then she sat down in front of the ultra-low frequency monitor. If her guess was right, she was about to get a show.

At two minutes before the listed sunrise, the needle pegged and drooped in modulated sound far beneath what she could hear, but Leslie had the same queasy dizziness she'd suffered through the day before. There seemed to be no pattern to the sounds, but there were defined ranges and intensities. *Ode to the sun? A buggy reveille call? What are my friends up to?*

At that moment, as the modulations crescendoed, Robbie called.

The shrill ring stopped the infrasound cold. Leslie grabbed the phone and yelled into it, "What!"

"Good morning to you, too. I hope you're only mad and not unhealthy."

"Oh, uh, Robbie, I'm fine, but you just broke in on something significant. New rule. Don't call me, I'll call you." Leslie subsided. "Look, I can't immerse myself here and do phone sex with you. Just leave me be, please."

"You sound rational for a change. Testy, but rational. Okay. Anything I can bring you?"

"No. Thanks. I've got a week's worth of food and water. And I think I might be getting closer. I'll keep calling you every day, promise."

"Okay, but also call me if you have any trouble— promise?"

"Sure. Enjoy the sunlight."

Leslie was desperate for stimulus. Life inside the coffin was an achingly boring sensory deprivation. She tried doing exercises, but only banged into the equipment. Then she fiddled with the ultra-low frequency monitor, greatly increasing its sensitivity, and noticed variations, faint recurring variations, as if orders were being sent out within the hive. *Get a grip, bitch. You don't need an anthropomorphic bias. Just record the data.*

But another idea struck her. She recorded the faint vibrations and retransmitted them back into the hive. The reaction was immediate. Soldier termites, mandibles snapping, swarmed onto the screen and started biting it. An acrid chemical smell billowed into the chamber. Leslie started coughing uncontrollably, and shut down the transmission. The soldiers held position for a few seconds, and then returned into the hive tunnels. The smell eventually dissipated and her hacking subsided as well.

Oh, ho, ho. Let's see if I can pick up the discovery tempo before I go stir crazy.

Leslie jacked in headphones and adjusted the sound frequency so she could hear the vibrations, put on the headphones, took her usual dose of acid, and settled down to see if she couldn't be force-fed bug speak.

It was a mistake. When she drifted into focus at three a.m., she screamed. The mesh screen between her and the termites had somehow slid back, and there was nothing holding the termites in the hive. And they'd migrated. No soldier termites that she noticed, but hordes of worker termites and even more white larvae, which the workers had presumably carried in.

Leslie kept screaming, but her hertz range was much higher than the insects could sense. She yanked herself into a sitting position and brushed off as many bugs as she could see on her clothes, but knew from the tingles that many more had found their way under her blouse and into her hair.

God damn! God damn! I must have pushed open the screen when I was drugged up. Got to get out of here.

But as she reached for the hatch, Leslie noticed that for all her bug coverage, she hadn't been bitten by soldier termites. She reached for the screen handle to slide it shut and paused. If she could bear it, she'd be living among the termites rather than next to them. She had a vague realization that the drugs had knocked her out of sanity, but didn't care. *Nearer my arthropodal God to thee. Me and my termite bros, No, listen closer. They have a plan for us. Pity I can't eat dead wood with them, I am what I eat, wait, wait.*

Leslie stared down at the dead and struggling termites that littered the floor of her coffin. *We are what we eat.* She knelt down and began picking up larva and workers one by one and dropping them into her mouth. *The workers are crunchy, but the larvae are like clotty oatmeal.*

She cleared enough floor space to sit down, casually picking termites off her clothes and eating them as she tried to think.

More acid, can't get through to them without my drug. Ah, that's better. Now, so close, let them know I'm here, I'm hearing, I'm home, mamma.

Leslie switched her equipment to broadcast into the hive and listened as soldiers crabbed over the window frame toward her.

171

Robbie found her seven hours later, when Leslie hadn't called and hadn't answered his call. Her body was so swollen it couldn't fit through the hatch, and the fire department had to cut a hole in the container roof. Leslie was misdiagnosed twice and almost died before they found that toxins from the soldier termites were poisoning her. It was four days before she regained an impaired consciousness and could talk to Robbie.

"You almost died, kid."

"I'm—you're—talk is hard funny. We will die."

"No you won't, Les. You're getting better."

"No, unbetter. Different. They sing to their gods in earthquake tones, Robbie. They see longer timed than us. We overbreed into the most food available. Before the millennium, we are sacrifice. We will be hunted. Watch for swarms."

Herstory

Alison McBain

LORI RECEIVED NOTIFICATION FOR THE first of May. She'd read somewhere that the term May Day was from the French *m'aider—help me*—but wasn't sure if that was true or another fiction from before the revolution.

May Day gave her a week to prepare, but she couldn't think of anything else she needed to do. The furniture was already in place, the bedding and clothing washed and stacked in neat rows in the drawers next to the crib. Everything sat shining and new in her spare bedroom, now painted a soft, pale pink.

A sharp cramp rippled down her spine—she'd received a packet of pills each month that was supposed to mask the symptoms of pregnancy and help eliminate possible defects, but each month she furtively washed the pills down the lavatory. She knew that if they found out, her name would be put on a list for readjustment. She'd have to go to counseling for hours on end and watch video after video about the revolution. The thought of seeing those events again, even secondhand, was enough to give her nightmares.

She'd lived through the horror of revolution, and while she'd never been assigned to cleanup detail, no one alive could have avoided seeing the aftermath of the engineered, airborne virus. The bodies just lying on the street or trapped in stationary cars and locked houses, waiting for burial. The haunting smell of rotted discards . . .

Only one fact had allowed her to avoid the grisly service of cleaning up the streets. She'd been one of many in counseling, one of the masses who had not even seen the revolution coming. Others like her had been grouped into readjustment classes in the initial effort to consolidate *Onenation* and move forward from an inescapable past.

Lori had been too scared to say anything but "yes" back then to the questions she was asked, her eyes blinded by the countless bodies on the streets.

Unfortunately, her neighbor Isabelle was more vocal. Whenever they didn't stopper Izzy's mouth, she screamed about her murdered children and the killers of her spouse. But Isabelle had vanished from the counseling center after just two weeks of treatment. Lori hadn't asked why, hadn't asked after her neighbor.

Had never seen her again.

So Lori could picture in great detail what would happen if she were caught. The steps they would take if she protested. What might happen to her baby if she failed the tests.

"Don't you want what's best for your baby? Best for Onenation?"

This pain she felt from not taking the pills was a defiance, a personal secret she held tightly to herself. It was the only part of this process that seemed uniquely hers. Everything else was heavily regulated. There were even words she wasn't allowed to say in the baby's hearing—words from before the revolution.

Patriarchy. Boy. Man.

Husband.

To be fair, they'd warned her about the rigor of the procedure when they'd contacted her as a likely candidate. Her appearance and medical history was deemed satisfactory—no flaws, no blemishes, no history of cancer or heart disease. A perfect record.

The interviewers had stressed the honor of being chosen, and how it would impact her future job evaluations. That she'd get an extra day of unmonitored vacation added to her allotment each year, as long as the child thrived.

When she'd even hesitated at that bribe, the lead interviewer dropped her voice half an octave. "You don't want to be seen as a *sympathizer*, do you?"

So she'd signed up. Lori hadn't expected that in this aspect of her compliance, even her body wouldn't belong to her anymore—instead, she was constantly monitored. The pills were the least of it. Each day, a set amount of exercise and a fixed diet. Any deviance would set off the alarms, and she'd be cautioned to adhere to the guidelines. All to protect the baby.

Although she'd heard horror stories about childbirth from twenty years ago—blood, ruptured parts, death—they didn't seem quite real, didn't seem immediate. Those things didn't happen anymore, and the stricture of the government's demands seemed excessive.

But, then again, a lot of things didn't happen anymore. Life was peaceful, even if sometimes she felt there was a space waiting to be filled. She remembered her father, her grandfather, her uncles—not everyone did, but she was old enough to remember them. Her two housemates, twenty and twenty-two respectively, were only babies when the revolution took place. But she was in her mid-thirties now, and she had grown up in the old regime. No matter how hard they tried, her memories couldn't be erased.

Since she'd become pregnant, she'd recently become wistful about doctors. Sometimes she wished for more than a blank screen looking back at her at the end of each checkup. From her childhood, she remembered lollipops given by Betty, the receptionist, and Dr. Henry with his solemn handshake at the end of each visit, the gentle gesture making her feel very grown up. The machines replaced doctors just a year or so after the revolution. Now, the process was safe, flawless. But it didn't stop her from dreaming for something she couldn't put a name to.

May Day morning dawned, and she left her apartment and walked towards the center of town. Electric trolleys hummed along the rails, but she much preferred stretching her own legs, even if her swollen ankles slowed her down. She exchanged awkward "Good mornings" with the few women out and about on the street, trying not to notice their eyes resting on her protruding stomach. Lori didn't want to see envy, and she was afraid to see the same ambivalence she felt on someone else's face.

If she did see someone who was conflicted, like her, would it change anything at all?

Women who aren't behind Onenation cause Onenation to fall behind. The motto plastered on every government building—Lori could salute that phrase in her sleep.

From far away, she could see other rounded figures converging on the main road from side streets and pointing unerringly north. A bus passed by, and the women in it looked down at her as she made her slow, shambling progress forward. Some of these women on the bus were headed to the hospital, she guessed. They had passed Onenation's tests, just like she had.

When Lori reached the hospital entrance, dozens of women were ahead of her, more quickly queuing up behind. They proceeded down the hall, and their footsteps echoed in the cheerfully bright corridor plastered with colorful posters. Lori saw the familiar government logo on half a dozen of the hangings: *Women who aren't behind Onenation cause Onenation to fall behind.* Their slippered feet whispered across the tiles of the corridor with the shushing sound of rain falling on leaves.

At the end of the hall was a kiosk guarding a closed set of doors. Each woman stopped, punched in their identity code, and the machine spat out a plastic bracelet with a barcode. The woman would slip it on her wrist, wave the barcode at the door, and it would open to admit her.

Lori followed procedure, and passed through the door into a large room that looked like an airline hanger. But instead of airplanes, it held rows and rows of padded tables with stirrups already extended in anticipation. Below the stirrups was a rounded tray, almost like a punch bowl, only three or four times the size and tilted slightly towards the head of each table. Each tray was padded with towels and blankets.

Lori hadn't realized there were so many of them who had volunteered for this next step in Onenation's progress. She pictured a few years in the future, her child reading about this in a lesson book and being proud of her mother for being a part of it.

The thought was humbling. The ambivalence she felt—had been feeling for months—eased slightly. She recalled the slight anticipation she'd had when signing up for the procedure, the hope for the future of Onenation. She felt tinged by the same emotion as she followed the line of women, walked nearly to the end of a middle row, and stopped at a table.

Nothing personalized the contraption where she would give birth. She glanced left and right and saw the other women were paying no attention to her. Side by side, they were sitting down on their tables and wriggling out of pants, skirts, dresses. The woman five spots up already had her blouse rucked up to her breasts and had lifted her legs into the stirrups, waiting.

Lori looked away, sat down on the table, and pulled down her pants and underwear. It felt odd, being exposed in such a large space. She lay down and stared up at the ceiling, her legs propped up like the other women, and thought about the weight of history that had led them to this point.

A robot trundled up, toting a plastic box of filled syringes. Lori watched as it scanned the bracelet of the woman next to her, gripped her arm with one pincer, and efficiently administered a shot in the crook of her elbow. A second robot followed behind, collecting the waste into a biohazard box as the first robot moved towards Lori's table. Before it was Lori's turn, she heard a faint wail and turned her head. The first woman of her row was already holding a baby.

So fast, she thought, and tensed for the needle.

The sting of contact was followed by a wave of pressure as her water broke. The pressure continued, followed by an infant arriving with efficient timing. The baby rocked gently into the waiting tray, and Lori quickly bent over to give her a quick swipe clean with the waiting towels. The baby began to cry as Lori wrapped her in a blanket.

Lori stared down, entranced at the waving hands, the screwed-up eyes, and open mouth. Smiling, she ran a hand down the girl's soft, fat cheek, as another series of robots came by to assist in cleaning up the afterbirth. But she paid them no attention—all her focus was on the little girl, the one who was hers. Taken from her genes, a perfect clone of what the government deemed a suitable candidate.

But, like the secret pain she had cherished, this girl was *hers*. Not theirs.

"Bracelet?"

Lori looked up. She hadn't been expecting a voice, not after the wordless dance of the mechanical assistants. It was a woman wearing the bright yellow uniform of government special services. Lori automatically held out her wrist for scanning, protectively cradling her baby in her other arm.

The officer gave a brisk nod as she read the results of Lori's scan. "Please place the infant back in the tray for inspection," she said.

"Inspection?" But then Lori snapped to attention. This final detail had been in the notification packet. "Oh, yes." She placed the baby in the tray.

The officer flipped open the wrapping covering her baby, and Lori bit her lip at the roughness of the gesture. She couldn't help her abortive reaching out as the officer grabbed the baby's legs in one hand and half-lifted her off the tray. The baby's face turned red with the intensity of her crying as the officer flipped her over to inspect her back.

Finally, the woman shook her head and wrapped up the infant again. Lori reached out in anticipation, but instead the officer picked up her baby and turned away. It was at that moment Lori saw the robotic cart waiting just behind her.

"What . . . what are you doing?" Lori asked as the officer wedged her baby in between two other newborns, both screaming. The cart must have been holding a dozen, with room for perhaps half a dozen more.

"Defective," the officer said. She glanced up over her scanner. "It happens sometimes, despite the testing and the medications. We calculated a point four percent fail rate."

"Defective?" Lori shook her head. "No. No, she was perfect." Her vision pitched sideways, as if she were drunk. Her arms were still outstretched to receive her baby, but she couldn't feel them anymore.

"Get dressed," the officer said coldly. Then, as an afterthought, "Thank you for your service." She turned to go to the next bed.

"No," Lori whispered, horrified. She tried to stand, but her legs failed, and she sprawled on the pavement. Her hands left bloody imprints as they slapped down to stop her fall, and the shock of the impact sent flashes of pain up her shoulders and into her skull. "No! Please, give me my baby."

Lori heard it, then—the other mothers calling out, their voices echoing in the cavernous room. Just like her.

"Please—you can't!"

"My baby!"

"Give her back!"

Their voices were weak with surprise and horror, like hers had been.

Lori drew in a deep breath. She released it with all the strength left in her, all the suppression she'd undergone since the revolution, all the times she had closed her mouth, bitten her lip, and turned away. Years of pain and loss found voice, and she screamed, "*Help me!*"

The mothers who had passed this final test by *Onenation* were carrying their babies out the door, but one or two turned back at Lori's raw cry. They saw her, saw what had happened to her, and their eyes slid past her desperation. Hands clutched at their bundles. The fertility shuttles would soon be carrying these mothers home with their babies, the ones without defect. The girls who were unblemished, like their mothers.

After the clinically efficient robots during the birthing process, the human attendants who came at Lori's cry were unwelcome. When she wouldn't stand, they hauled her up by each arm. When she wouldn't walk, they pulled at her until she had no choice but to follow.

Lori glanced back over her shoulder one last time as they dragged her through a door that led farther into the hospital complex. She had made her final protest. It had failed, and she doubted she would ever pass back.

At the far door where they had first come in, Lori's last glimpse of the room was of the mothers leaving. Each of them cradled in their arms the new generation of Onenation— hundreds of babies born that morning. Girls identical in almost every way. Girls who were fatherless . . . and perfect.

Smell the Rain

Alex Giannini

I WAS IN THE LIVING room with the desk lamp on, watching TV. There was a noise like a paintbrush makes on a canvas coming from the bedroom to my left, and I turned and looked up at the horror that was dangling from my ceiling.

The white-hot flash of whatever it is that runs through your insides when you're absolutely terrified did its thing and ran through my insides, sending a flush of heat that settled in my stomach.

The bedroom was dark, with a streak of orange coming in through the blinds. But the nightmare on the ceiling was clear as day—it was all legs and coarse hairs and teeth and drool. It was abject horror come to life in my bedroom, is what it was, and I couldn't do anything but look at it.

And then it was gone.

Shot across the ceiling in a flash, to the other side of the room—the side of the bedroom that was blocked from my view by the door. Out of sight, but not even close to being out of mind.

So I sat there, feeling like the world was pressing down on my shoulders and pinning me to my corner of the couch. I could hear the thing on my bedroom ceiling clatter its teeth, or clean its claws, or talk to some other, unseen fiend up there on Planet What The Fuck is Going On.

It's funny. My first clear-headed thought stuck on the couch was to lament the fact that my cell phone sat uselessly in the bedroom, charging on the nightstand in the far corner of the room—in the monster's corner of the room.

Guess I wasn't gonna Tweet this out.

It's crazy. I know it's crazy. Bat-shit, stick-me-in-a-small-room crazy. But there was a giant spider-beast clicking and clacking and waiting for me in my bedroom. Now, full disclosure? I was probably more than a little high at the time. I'd had a couple buddies over earlier in the night and we smoked a bowl while we shot the shit and listened to some music.

But listen—I can handle my shit, man, and I've been getting high since high school and not once—Not. Once.— have I ever seen a nightmare creature materialize on my ceiling. And, swear to Whatever, I wasn't even feeling buzzed. That had vanished when my ex texted something evil and my brain filtered any and all Nice Things out and replaced it instead with Rage.

And that's when I realized it. The trick to this whole thing. The reason for being, if you will. Not mine. His. Its. Whatever.

That crazy-ass spider-thing on my ceiling? It was simply the physical manifestation of the Rage I felt inside at that particular moment. It had come to glorious, horrible life, right there on the ceiling in my bedroom. The anger and the pain and the frustration I felt? Apparently, all of that looks, literally, like a giant hell beast.

So I'd learned a couple of things. First and foremost among them—my innermost feelings could materialize in the real world, and I could create nightmare beasts from them. If you're a certain type of person, I know what you're thinking at this point. But no, my Happy Thoughts do not have the ability to manifest. Only the Bad Thoughts.

So this, as you can see, has put me at somewhat of an impasse.

The gift—yes, gift—to construct nightmares in the real world is one that I do not take lightly. That said, I've come to realize that I am a negative person by nature. And that... well, that has had *repercussions*.

Walking down the street earlier this week, there was a horde of giant, winged monsters tearing apart the architectural heritage of downtown.

In the corner office next to my shitty little cubicle at the shitty little office where I work, my boss was, quite viciously, ripped apart by a gaggle of black-clad vampires. (Not the sparkly kind, mind you. These were of the fuck-you-we're-ancient-and-terrifying ilk. Because, apparently, my inner thoughts are old-world-rooted in their desire for revenge.)

On my way home, the Uber driver who just wouldn't stop talking to me despite the fact that I was very clearly—and, initially, anyway—very politely buried in my iPhone met a fate I'd rather not speak of.

So at this point you might be asking: Why would I allow such horrible things to happen? The answer, as answers should be, is quite straightforward.

I simply assumed I was going mad.

When the spider-beast appeared on my ceiling, I convinced myself that I was stoned. When the vampires swarmed around my boss and left nothing of him save a rib or two, I simply assumed that I had gone, completely and utterly, insane. And when the liquid bits of the Uber driver were, finally, cleaned off the dashboard, I rationalized it away as one of those lucid dreams I used to read about in the Spiritual section of the bookstore.

But now I'm not so sure. Now, I think I might *not* be insane. Now, I'm terrified.

Because this morning I walked down to the parking lot attached to my shitty apartment building, and there was a shiny, black, newish sedan sitting where my 175,000-miles-gone CRV used to be, an "Uber" sticker clearly displayed in its windshield. And when I checked my Twitter feed at a red light, everyone was talking about the "construction damage" that occurred at lunchtime on Monday and these blurry-but-definitely-something photos popped up all over the Internet. And when I got to work, my boss still wasn't in his office, and no one had heard from him in three days. In my pocket, there's this sharp little piece of something a lot like bone that I keep turning, over and over again, in my left hand.

So now I've decided to do, probably, the stupidest thing I could possibly do. I've decided to write it all down, sitting here in a coffee shop, click-clacking away on the brand-new laptop I found in my bag when I sat down.

There were people in here when I came through the door. People at tables, talking about work and kids, and that one couple talking too loudly about how the dude had cheated again. There were people behind the counter. The nice girl who handed me my regular without even asking what I wanted. The cooks clanking their pots and their pans in the unseen kitchen area.

Now, though . . .

Now, there's no one else here, and it's just me, typing away in the back corner at a little barstool and table. There's a strong, mostly black drink with some foam on top of it sitting here next to me, and I don't think I like it very much. It's bitter and I'm still tired.

This may be how it all begins. Or ends, I mean. You know what I mean. Someone has to, right? The autosave feature keeps popping up on this laptop. I have no idea where this is being stored. The computer's not mine. I have no idea how I knew the password—Bradbury2112!—with a capitol B and an exclamation point at the end. It was just in my head.

I see something to my right, a shadow stalking just beyond the bar that splits the coffee shop into two parts. Around the corner, something bad is happening. In the kitchen, there are sounds like splashing water. I'm fairly certain it's my fault, whatever is happening. It's the anxiety. The fear. It's manifesting.

People are dying again, I think. That's definitely blood on the concrete floor. It's so quiet in here. Zeppelin was playing earlier over the speakers, "Ramble On." He was right.

And now it's time for me to go.

Acknowledgements

A collection of such marvelous stories like this is never the work of one person, and so I would like to take a moment to extend a hearty thank you to a number of people who helped this book arrive at publication.

First of all, thank you to the tireless folks at WestportWRITES, Cody Daigle-Orians and Alex Giannini. Due to their creativity and organization, they gathered together and ran the program that inspired the wonderful authors who have graced these pages.

In addition, a hearty thank you to all the authors and presenters of the many amazing programs sponsored by WestportWRITES, without whom this anthology would not have been possible.

Special thanks go out to the artists who have made this book as lovely as the words of the stories are powerful. The fabulous cover and back cover artist is Shannon Stamey. Interior chapter art was created by different talented artists from Pixabay.com, including Gordon Johnson (chapter images for "Herstory," "Monstrous Practices," and "Valley Girls") and Rachel Bostwick (chapter image for "Smell the Rain").

This book would not exist without all of you.

About the Authors

Edward Ahern

Edward Ahern sometimes detours into literary fiction and poetry, but he's best known as an innovative genre writer. He's tucked away several awards and honorable mentions for over two hundred poems and stories and five books. The stories have appeared in ten countries and, counting reprints, over three hundred publications. His stories can be listened to through Audible and the New York Public Library. And he started writing fiction at sixty-seven.

His editorial skills are based on a degree in journalism from the University of Illinois and extensive experience at the *Providence Journal*. Ed's been honing the skills for several years at *Bewildering Stories*, where he serves on the review board and as review editor with a staff of five. (*Bewildering Stories* is widely known for the author-friendly quality of its critiques.)

He has his original wife, but advises that after more than fifty years together they are both out of warranty. Two children and five grandchildren serve as affection focus and money drain.

His work career after university has been an enjoyably demented hopscotch game. U.S. Navy officer (diver and bomb disarmer); reporter for the *Providence Journal*; intelligence officer living in Germany and Japan; international sales and marketing executive at a Canadian paper company (twenty-three years, seventy four countries visited, MBA from NYU); same job for the company that also owns the New England Patriots; and retirement into writing like hell to make up for lost time.

Elizabeth Chatsworth

Elizabeth Chatsworth is a British author and actor based in Connecticut. She writes of rogues, rebels, and renegades across time and space. From Victorian sensibilities to interstellar travel, her fiction takes you on an adventure like no other!

Elizabeth is the author of THE BRASS QUEEN, an award-winning sci-fi comedy set in an alternate Victorian age. Her novelette "Ten Minutes After Teatime" is included in the Amazon bestseller *When to Now: A Time Travel Anthology*. A 2018 RWA® Golden Heart® finalist, Pitch Wars alumna, and Authors Guild member, Elizabeth is represented by Natalie Grazian of Martin Literary Management.

To be the first to receive exclusive news, sneak previews, and fabulous giveaways, please visit www.elizabethchatsworth.com.

Gabi Coatsworth

Gabi Coatsworth is an award-winning British-born writer and blogger, who has spent half her life living in the United States. Her essays, short fiction and poetry have been published in anthologies (*When to Now* and *Tangerine Tango: Women Writers Share Slices of Life*), E-chook's literary memoir app, and literary journals, both in print and online. You can find her blog for writers, and her personal blog, online at www.gabicoatsworth.com. Her memoir is currently with editors and now she is working on a women's fiction novel.

She lives in Connecticut, where she writes and runs groups for local authors, when she's not exploring other countries. All her social media accounts are under her name.

Cody Daigle-Orians

Cody Daigle-Orians writes plays and short stories. His full-length science fiction drama *18 Victoria* was published this spring by WriteForTheStage Books, and his work has appeared in *Strange Stories, Aphotic Realm, The GPTC Reader* and *The Best American Short Plays of 2015-2016.*

Dave D'Alessio

Dave D'Alessio is an ex-industrial chemist, ex-TV engineer, and ex-award-winning animator current masquerading as a social scientist. He is based in Bridgeport. His work has appeared in venues including *Daily Science Fiction, Heroic*

Fantasy Quarterly, and *Mad Scientist Journal*; his story "Twenty-Year Reich" was a finalist for the Sidewise Award in Alternative History fiction.

Alex Giannini

Alex Giannini is the author of the children's book, *Sarah Faire and the House at the End of the World*. He has written nonfiction titles for Bearport Publishing, and was a writer/producer at WWE.com.

Roman Godzich

Roman Godzich is a polyglot who has lived and worked in several countries. He has worked in ecommerce for more than 30 years and has designed e-commerce solutions, search engines, advertising platforms and online booking engines. He currently manages content and user experience for an online travel company.

He grew up in Manhattan and attended the Bronx High School of Science and New York University. He currently resides in Connecticut.

When not working or writing, Roman enjoys deep sea fishing, reading, and gourmet cooking.

Sheryl Kayne

Sheryl Kayne is an award winning writer, children's book author, book ghostwriter, storyteller and former StandUp comic. Four of her books are included in the Westport Library's collection: *Immersion Travel USA: The Best & Most Meaningful Volunteering, Living & Learning Excursions,* recipient of the Society of American Travel Writers Foundation's Lowell Thomas Travel Journalism Award in Best Travel Guidebook category, and *Volunteer Vacations Across America*, named on Amazon's List of Best New Travel Books; along with children's books, *Queen of the Kisses* and *Queen of the Kisses Meets Sam Under a Soup Pot.* Stay tuned: August 2019 for her newest children's book, *Terror in Texas*, part of the Scary States Series by Bearport Publishing. Currently at work on a series of mystery thrillers, children's books, and nonfiction, she's thrilled to be included in the Frankenstein anthology *Imagining Monsters* with her contribution: "A Conversation Between Mother and Son."

P.C. Keeler

Born in the far-off days of the Second Millennium, P.C. Keeler spends his days writing detailed instructions for very dim but precise silicon brains to follow and finds it a relaxing change of pace to write more conversationally for charming, handsome, intellectual readers like you. He enjoys past, present, and future, preferably all at once. Steampunk and Ren Faires work well for this.

Currently residing in the wilds of Fairfield County, Connecticut, he grew up in New Hampshire and as such has never quite gotten used to sales tax. His first published work was a short poem printed by a local newspaper at the tender age of six. Him, that is. The newspaper was considerably more well-established. He has continued writing since, including the YA science fiction novel *Migon*. His most recent publication was in the Fairfield Scribes' award-winning anthology *When To Now* with "Try Again."

When not writing code at the day job, writing fiction after hours, or visiting Ren Faires in a vacuum-tube-bedecked top hat, P.C. can be found trying frantically to catch up on sleep. He is pondering a trip into Mad Science simply so as to be able to build a device to slow the rotation of the planet and create the 28-hour day for this purpose. Donations welcome.

Alison McBain

Diversity is one of Alison McBain's passions. With dual Canadian-U.S. citizenship, a Japanese-American mother and a B.A. in African history and classical literature, she has an eclectic background and a wide range of experience. She grew up in California and moved to the East Coast in her mid-twenties, finally settling in Connecticut to raise her three daughters.

She started her writing career at age four with a "self-published" horror story about the monster in the closet. The story was highly lauded by her closest family members. Since then, she's received a number of writing awards and accolades from people not even vaguely related to her, but she still has a soft spot for that first short story.

Her interest in diversity also extends to fiction. With nearly a hundred short publications to her name, her stories and poems range in tone from serious to silly. Her work covers nearly every genre, including literary, romance, horror, science fiction, fantasy, history and adventure. As an author, she has one novel (*The Rose Queen*) and one short story collection (*Enchantress of Books*) under her belt. She was also lead editor for three anthologies (*When to Now: A Time Travel Anthology*, *Imagining Monsters*, and *Don't Be a Hero: a VILLAINthology*), and was recently nominated for the Pushcart Prize for poetry.

When not writing fiction, she follows her own personal mantra of, "Do something creative every day." Once in a while, she puts on her Book Reviews Editor hat for the magazine *Bewildering Stories,* pens a webcomic about parenting called *Toddler Times*, and interviews creatives on her website www.alisonmcbain.com. When life gets a little too hectic, she does origami meditation or draws all over the walls of her house with the enthusiastic help of her kids.

V.P. Morris

V.P. Morris is an award-winning horror and thriller writer. She is the host of the suspenseful audio drama, *The Dead Letters Podcast*, debuting in August 2019. When she isn't working on her latest manuscript, she is reviewing thriller novels and horror movies on social media. You can follow her @teawriterepeat on Twitter and Instagram.

Marc Sirkin

Marc Sirkin is from a faraway, and yet not so distant land called "Corporate," and has spent the past two decades trying to figure out how to avoid shaving, traffic, and meetings. Two out of three ain't bad! He's recently completed a short play, a YA/sci-fi novel, a personal memoir, and several short stories. Marc attended Florida State University and the Art Institute of Atlanta, and when not in meetings, he's watching or reading things that feature flaming swords, kung-fu fighting, or characters in tight spandex costumes.

Corinne "Mitzy Sky" Taylor

Corrine "Mitzy Sky" Taylor shares her journey through writing, spoken word, and videography. She's consciously unlearning messages that prevented her from living wholeheartedly. Her children, and young people experiencing adversities, have been the motivations to share the human resilience spirit of rising above difficult life circumstances. She is grateful to have friends that are supportive, hold her accountable to do her best, and believe in her. She uses the gifts she received from her grandmother, the life lessons that she learned, and being a voracious reader of books from people who have gone through great adversity but find their way through, and shares with others to never give up. She also enjoys the occasional reading of mystery, crime drama, and sci-fi.

Growing up without television and mostly living outdoors, she saw her first movie *True Grit* with John Wayne on the big screen as a child in Jamaica and became fascinated on how it came to be. After much curiosity, she learned how to film and video edit at the Soundview public television station in Bridgeport, Connecticut. She did an on-job-training with Emmy Award winning producer Frank Borres at American View Productions. She created the Beyond the Story workshop that she facilitates at conferences, and developed the Compassionate Activism training at Advocacy Unlimited (AU), where she works in advocacy education and outreach. Her writing has been published at *Mad in America* online website, the *Inner-City News*, and she writes a blog for the AU newsletter. Her life experiences have guided her to write *I Am Not Your Mental Patient: A Glimpse at What Forgiveness Can Do,* and start a video and writing blog www.mitzysky.com or www.iamnotyourmentalpatient.com.

D.J. Whitney

D.J. Whitney is an author, screenwriter, musician, filmmaker, and actor who resides in Connecticut. He spent several years writing a wide array of screenplays. A few still in the works and some over time reviewed by Hollywood studios. His stories, concepts, and dialogue were always well-received but the critiques were dependent on who read the scripts. Each review motivates and inspires him to keep writing, learning, and strengthening characters, words, and ideas.

Presently in his creative journey, he is driven to writing novels. His weaving of poignant life lessons and pieces of authentic characters he has met along the road not only is evident throughout his stories, but also creates inspirational characters and relatable stories.

He is elated, to say the least, to be included in *Imagining Monsters* with an excerpt from his novel "Hairwolf."

For more information about the authors, including their forthcoming publications, interviews, and how to get in contact with them, please visit the Fairfield Scribes' website at www.fairfieldscribes.com.